MAGIC CALLS

ECHOES BOOK ONE

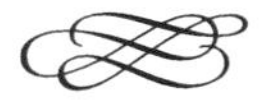

MIRIAM GREYSTONE

* * *

Be sure to join my Insiders list to get free sneak peeks, new release notices, and giveaways! Join here: http://www.miriamgreystone.com/connect-with-me/

Molly's story continues in Magic Cries . . .

Magic Cries

Available now on Amazon!!
http://www.miriamgreystone.com/getbook2

For Rachel

Love you always, Sis.

MOLLY

Molly clutched the microphone in slick palms, waiting for the right chord, the right millisecond, to fall back into song. She breathed in the smoke-stained air deeply, like it was perfume. She wasn't even high; she marveled as the beat pulsed inside her. Life was just this good.

The music swelled, and she let the words flow through her lips. Small and slightly shabby, the Homeland Bar wasn't built for large crowds. But the people kept streaming in, pushing the scratched-up wooden tables against the walls, standing on top of the pool tables, jostling one another as they tried to get a little closer to the stage. People hurrying by on the street heard a strain of music and suddenly stopped to listen. A minute later, they were pushing in through the bar's propped-open door, shoving inside until the whole place seemed to breathe in and out like one giant, sweating creature; the pounding drums the heartbeat they all shared.

Intermission came, and it seemed wrong to let the music fade. But Molly's band needed a break. The crowd gave a collective sigh of disappointment as Molly stepped away from the microphone and twisted open a bottle of water. Then they started chatting and moving toward the bar to get a drink. Mike put down his guitar and waved to Molly before he hopped down from the stage and went to grab another beer. It was his fourth, but she still considered it a success: it meant he hadn't hit the hard stuff yet. She drained her bottle of water and walked over, grinning, to where Tim sat at the drums.

"Amazing show, bro!" she crowed, wrapping her arms around him in a powerful bear hug. He was so wide across the shoulders and thick in the middle she could barely hold him. "It's been unbelievable tonight!"

"Piss off," Tim said mildly, shoving her away. "And I'm not your brother—don't call me that. If you do, there'll be weirdness when we start sleeping together."

"So, what? You'd rather be more in the category of cousin? Neighbor?"

"I am in the category of best damn drummer in this freaking town. And you fall into the category of very lucky to have me. There are dozens of bands within just a few miles of here who would kill to have me on stage with them."

"We might be able to arrange that, actually," said Molly, tapping her chin. "If they put their stages next to ours, you could probably be on several all at once."

"Abuse me if you like. We all know who the minions really come to see." He turned to face the bar, raising both his fists in the air. "I AM AWESOME!" His face turned bright red as he bellowed, and a few people hooted and cheered. He turned back to his drum set.

"See what I mean? Honestly, any day now, you're going to give up this coy act and fall into bed with me."

"No way, Tim!" Janice stumbled up from behind and threw an unsteady arm around Molly's shoulder. "Molly's only got eyes for Hot-Front-Row-Guy." Her head swayed back and forth as she surveyed the crowd. "Where is Hot-Front-Row-Guy, anyway?"

"Janice?" Molly said, smelling the licorice and liquor on her breath. "How trashed are you?"

"Moderately trashed," Janice replied, wrapping her arms around Molly's waist and resting her head on Molly's shoulder.

"We've talked about this. Many, many times," Molly reminded her.

"Yes! And I have broken none of your rules, oh great one!" Janice giggled. "I remember everything you said," she counted off on her fingers. "You said I had to be able to sing, and play, and stay conscious until the end of the show. No problem!" She leaned in to whisper in Molly's ear. "I've got a good reason to stay conscious tonight. Look over at the bar. See the bald guy? That's Danny. He's with me!"

Molly felt her eyebrows arch as she looked at the bald man at the bar. He was a biker for sure, at least two feet taller than Janice and three times her bulk. Possibly also twice her age. Janice was super slender, with pale white skin and black curly hair, and was so short she often got carded at the bars they played in. She seemed to feel the need to compensate by pairing up with large, burly men who could smash anyone who bothered her. The problem was that Janice displayed such consistently lousy taste in men that they often ended up smashing her as well.

"You could come out with us after the show," Janice giggled. "He's got lots of hot friends, and they all ride badass motorcycles and wear leather jackets. You'd have fun, I promise!"

"I'll think about it," Molly said, wanting to shut her up, and ignoring Tim's exaggerated howl of indignation in the background. If nothing else, it would give her a way to keep an eye on Janice.

"You really should come," Janice coaxed. "Your special friend hasn't been in the front row for a couple of weeks, right?"

Molly untangled herself from Janice's embrace and straightened up. She pulled her long brown hair, streaked with vivid red, into a messy ponytail.

"Jake isn't a special friend. He's just a guy who used to come to our concerts."

"Right," Janice nodded. "Just a guy who came. And when he was here, all of a sudden, you were always singing just to him, and he would stand right there and stare up at you. And then you two would have all those long, private chats after the concert. Where'd he disappear to, anyway?"

"Haven't a clue," Molly shrugged, her eyes darting to the spot in the front row where Jake used to stand. "He was going downhill pretty fast. Maybe he shot up all the heroin in DC and had to go somewhere else to find more. Now, seriously, give me a cigarette," she held out her hand. "And don't tell me you don't have any. I smelled them on your breath."

"So that's how it is, huh?" Janice pouted, digging a Marlboro from her pocket. "You think that just 'cause you head up the band, you get to demand cigarettes?" She dangled the cigarette in the air. "What's in it for me?"

Molly grabbed it and tucked it into her pocket.

"How about you get to sing the lead for the next number?"

"Really?"

"Yeah, your voice is perfect for that one. Go for it."

"Deal! I've got to tell Danny. He'll be blown away!" Janice ran toward the burly man at the bar with a huge grin plastered across her face.

Molly stripped her leather jacket from her shoulders and carefully lay it down on top of Tim's drum case. It was frigid outside, but on stage, the lights pressed against her skin like an affectionate, warm hand, and she loved to leave her shoulders bare in the bright light. There were no bruises there now, no ugly purple marks left by cruel, crushing fingers. She gloried in the silky-smooth perfection of her skin; in the way that flesh can heal. The marks that wouldn't go away weren't even visible now. Some were covered by the thick bracelets she wore, and others were swallowed up by her tattoo. The skeleton key drawn in ink on her shoulder wove into and around the scar, transforming it. Now it was just part of what made her strong. Fearless.

She stepped down off the stage, weaving through the throngs of people. The bartender smiled and tossed her another bottle of water before she even asked. Molly smiled her thanks and leaned against the bar, watching the people laughing and talking around her as she gulped it down.

"It's too dangerous," a voice at her elbow said. Molly started and turned toward the young woman standing at her side.

"I'm sorry. What did you say?"

"What you're doing. It's too dangerous. You've got to stop it. Like, right now."

The girl looked too old to be in high school, but not by much. Her wide brown eyes and doe-like expression made Molly want to wrap an arm around her thin shoulders and tell her that everything would be alright. Her loose black curls were cut short but still slid into her eyes. Her skin was light brown, and her cheekbones and nose were sprinkled thickly with freckles.

"You've got to realize it, right? You know that you're taking a terrible risk."

"What are you talking about?" For a second, Molly wondered if the kid was some sort of missionary, but the girl's torn jeans and threadbare hoodie didn't quite look the part. "I think you must have me mixed up with someone else. Are *you* alright? Because you seem kind of freaked out."

"You don't understand," the girl hissed and wrapped her fingers around Molly's wrist.

Instantly, an instinct surged in Molly to pull back, to strike out. She stiffened, then pulled in a deep breath that hissed through her teeth, forcing herself to relax. This wide-eyed child was no threat to her.

"They are watching you," the girl said, and Molly forced herself to focus on her words, feeling worry unfurl in her chest. She knew what fear looked like, and this girl, who clutched Molly's arm while her eyes darted around the room, was petrified. "I've got to get out of here," the girl whispered, almost to herself. "This was a mistake. I never should have come here." She brought her eyes up to focus on Molly's face. "But if you're smart, you won't get back up on that stage. Go out the back. Run as fast as you can and don't ever come back."

Then the girl spun around, pushing her way through the crowd, moving toward the door.

"I can't do that!" Molly called out after her, but the girl didn't turn back. Molly cursed under her breath, pushing through the throng, trying to catch up with her. Whatever the girl had been talking about, she was in trouble. Molly would have liked to see if there was some way she could help.

But the girl was gone.

"Molly, come on! We've got to start the second set," Janice called out. For a moment, Molly stood, still staring at the churning crowd, hoping the girl would come back. But she was gone. Sighing, Molly pushed her thoughts away. There would always be some degree of craziness that came with being a performer. People would come up to her and say all kinds of weird things; she couldn't let it spook her. She sipped deeply from her water bottle as she wove through the crowd and climbed back up to the stage. Janice followed, grinning at Molly impishly as she took the microphone in her hands and began the next song. The music thrummed back to life. The crowd was still milling around, getting one more drink, checking their phones, while Janice's voice, sweet and bell-like, rang out above them. Molly rolled her head from side to side, stretching while she let everything except the music fall away. Then she threw her arm around Janice's shoulder and leaned in to sing back-up, not caring if the audience was paying attention or not.

It had taken such a long time—so many months, so many small steps—to build up the band and rebuild her life. But she had done it. She had made it this far. This bar had become more than just a place to share her music—it had practically become her home. Molly could hear her voice, intertwining with Janice's as she sang. Her voice was stronger; the tones truer than they had ever been before. She felt free.

The crowd clustered back around the stage, staring up at Molly, their faces eager; vulnerable. Janice finished her song and, with a little wave toward the bar, moved aside to let Molly take center stage.

The music ramped back up, and Molly felt her heart rate building to match the frantic beat that Tim was pounding on the drums.

She caught herself scanning the crowd, looking for Jake's burning eyes staring up at her, wishing he was there, sharing the high that came with the music. But, deep down, Molly had known for a long time she was losing him to a different high, one stealing his life away right before her eyes. A feeling of loss swelled inside her, and then her words burned as they came, rasping in her throat as they poured out faster and freer. She sang song after song, the intensity growing until the whole place was swelling with it, the music a building pressure against eardrums and heart.

This was who she was, all she wanted, the most amazing thing she could imagine. She sang and wept and screamed. People pressed against each other, straining to get near her, reaching their arms, shouting and yelling. Wanting her. She gave and gave to them, holding nothing back. But the more she poured herself out, the more she felt full; the more she gave, the more she felt like bursting. Molly hunched over the microphone, letting the words crash out of her like her soul was pouring into the microphone, reverberating through the air. She clenched her eyes shut and sang of a heart broken and remade but still, somehow, not nearly whole.

The first thing she noticed, the first thing that reached her through the haze and the frenzy and the joy of the music, was that the beat was missing.

Tim's drumming had stopped.

Molly kept singing. The song was pushing against her from the inside, and she needed to release it into the air. Then Janice's voice faltered and was silent. Mike struck the wrong chord on his guitar, and the speakers screamed in protest. The music halted.

Molly's words died in her throat, and she opened her eyes. No one moved.

The whole bar rang with silence.

The bar was full of hundreds of dirty, sweat-stained people, all of them pumped up, many drunk.

No one spoke.

Molly swung around, looking to her band—her friends—trying to understand what was happening, trying to fight the panic rising like a tsunami inside her, the inexplicable feeling she had done something. Something terribly wrong. But Janice stared at her, frozen and unmoving, her eyes strangely vacant and her hands loose at her sides, her jaw slack. Tim, sitting behind his drum set, was staring at Molly, his eyes piercing, like he was looking deep inside her, at some part of herself that she didn't recognize, and didn't want to own.

The crowd was motionless. Someone's cell phone rang, but no one answered.

They all stood, looking at her. Every single person in the bar was staring at her with something wild in their eyes that frightened Molly.

It reminded her of hunger.

Fear, sharp and unexpected, surged inside her. She stepped back, away from all those eyes staring up at her. Away from all those blank, upturned faces.

Moving together, as though they were all one, every person in the bar took a single, slow step toward her.

Molly gasped. What had she done? She felt like a child who, pretending to drive a parent's car, accidentally pushed a button and brought something rumbling to life she didn't understand and couldn't hope to control. She felt the silence around her like a physical presence, felt the expectation, the demand for it, to be filled.

She trembled.

She looked out at the sea of blank, empty faces. And toward the back of the bar, something moved. She saw a flash of blue eyes and the curl of a smile on a darkly shadowed face. But somehow, the glimpse of that face scared her just as much as the bar's eerie silence.

A familiar instinct flared inside her. Spinning toward the back door, her feet sprang into motion, and she did what came naturally.

Molly ran.

JAKE

It burned. The pain was a knife, twisting deep in Jake's gut; he stumbled as he hurried. His insides contracted, and he stopped, leaning against a wall in the darkness. He would have thrown up if there had been any food in his system; instead, the dry heaves racked him from his core.

He was dying.

He had known for a while that the drugs were killing him. He had wished, more than once, that they would hurry up and get the job done. This time he had woken from his blackout in a backroom bathroom that belonged to people whose names he did not even know, with piss stains on his clothes and a stench on the outside he imagined almost matched the putrid rot of his soul. He couldn't stand it. Couldn't stand the need, the pain. Couldn't stand himself. He didn't care if he died; he hoped he would. But he needed to be high again. Now.

Jake paused and squinted against the blurriness that clouded his eyes. Just over a block away, he could see the bar door propped open, the glow from inside spilling out into the street. He was too far away to really hear, but the memory of her music echoed in his mind. He wanted to turn, to walk toward the light and the life.

Toward Molly. But he knew what he looked like, understood what he was. He didn't belong there.

He knew where he had to go.

The docks weren't too far, but getting there wasn't his only problem. His friends had done him the favor of emptying his pockets while he was on the nod. But Jake had discovered during the last few years that everybody needs something—even dealers. It wouldn't be the first time that he'd been on his knees.

What do you need? What do I have to do? I'll do it. I'll do it. Just give it to me. Give it to me. Anything. Anything. Anything.

He stumbled along, pausing when his legs threatened to give out. He stood outside a parking garage. Metal steps spiraling upwards into an empty, cement tomb. Fluorescent lighting. Jake looked up at it for a long moment, hope sparking inside him. He turned and forced himself to climb the steps.

He spotted a white four-door Nissan that had clearly seen better days, parked off to the side, in the shadows. He grabbed a piece of concrete from a crumbling parking barrier nearby. Wrapping his hand carefully in his sleeve, he punched in the window.

What a waste.

Feverishly Jake dug through the glove compartment, rooted around in the back. Nothing. Nothing except a shitty GPS. His hands shook as he pocketed it. There had to be something better.

Stumbling as he moved, he finally found a freshly washed BMW on the third level. He was so excited when he found it he forgot to wrap his hand before he smashed the glass. It came back all bloody, and a flying shard scraped against his cheekbone. He didn't care—he liked the pain. This pain was clean; satisfying. He could see the wound, feel the blood trickle through his fingers. It was so much better than the burn the drugs left behind. This pain cleared his head and steadied him, so with a sure hand, Jake quickly searched the car. Credit cards, iPad, and a watch that was worth at least a hundred, even on the streets. One hundred and seventy-two dollars in cash. It would be more than enough. He turned and stumbled back down the stairs.

He smelled it before he saw it, the freshness that rolled off the waves mixed with the rankness of seafood left, rotting, in crates next to the shore. The docks were silent, the water like smooth black glass, the lamplight that reflected off it staring back at Jake like ghostly, yellow eyes. He walked slower now, being cautious. The docks appeared deserted, but Jake's practiced eye saw what others would miss. Before long he spotted one of his regular guys, squatting in the darkened doorway of a waterside restaurant. They made the deal quick enough.

Just the sound of the foil packet, crinkling in his hand, made him feel better. Jake peeked inside, making sure that the precious powder was enough. He turned, wondering if he should try to make it home, or find a cozy spot in a dark doorway and settle in for the night.

The first blow caught him squarely in the back of the head, knocking him so hard that he blacked out for a second and woke just as his face slammed into the cement. The blood in Jake's mouth was wet and bitter; he spat it out and roared in shock and rage. He felt the syringe in his front pocket snap, and the foil slipped from his hand. He tried to turn over, determined to tear his attacker limb from limb, and a second blow hit him hard on the side.

"Easy, easy!" he heard a voice call out. "We need him in fighting condition!"

Suddenly he felt weight on top of him. Someone was sitting on his back. His arms were being pulled behind him and fastened tightly together, so tightly that he could feel hard plastic binding cutting into his skin.

"WHAT THE HELL ARE YOU DOING?" he screamed, rage making lights pop behind his eyes.

"Watch that temper, boy!" a mild voice said behind him, and then his ankles were bound.

"I'LL FUCKING KILL YOU!" Jake roared, but the only response was laughter. Jake saw the lamplight shimmering weakly on the foil envelope just inches away. Even at that moment, more than anything else, he wished his hands were free so he could hold it. Caress it. But then a hood was pulled over his eyes, and all he saw was blackness.

JAKE

Jake was still conscious when they threw him in the van. He heard the metal doors swing open. They hoisted him into the air and flung him roughly inside, so that as he landed, he slammed his face full force into the van floor. For a while, his yelling was muffled by the blood in his mouth and the confusion in his mind. Periodically, he would strain uselessly against his bonds, or try to shake off the hood. The hood blinded him, and its blackness faded in and out, impossible to distinguish from the moments when his eyes rolled back into his head, and a different darkness descended.

Suddenly, he was fourteen years old, riding in the backseat with Mary. It was dark out, but Mom was still driving. They had moved slower than they'd meant to, like always, and even though it was late, they still had at least an hour more of driving till they reached their new place. Mom kept yelling back at them to go to sleep already; she was sick of their squabbling, and they were giving her a headache. Jake didn't care, he knew the real reason for his mother's headache. Besides, he liked nestling down on the seat with Mary, a flashlight held between them, whispering and laughing and occasionally punching each other in the ribs.

When reality flashed back, and he realized where he was, tears mixed with the blood that trickled down his face. If only he really could go back. Try again. That had been when things were good—the time between towns, between jobs, when it seemed possible that, just like Mom promised, the new life they were headed to really would be better than the one they'd left behind. She really had tried at first but, just like always, it wore off after a month or two. But even then, he had still had Mary. She would smile at him when he got back from school, sit at the kitchen table and help him with his homework. They spent hours playing video games together. Life felt almost happy.

But when Mary left, even the little good he had turned sour.

"I *have* to go, Jake," she said the night before she left, packing her suitcase and looking at him apologetically as he stood hunched against her door frame. The job she had been hoping and waiting for had finally come through, a secretarial position at the state university. She could take classes for free, at night, and work toward a degree. "I have to get out of here. Mom will make me lose my mind if I stick around any longer. But I know you. I know how tough you are. And in three years you'll be done with school, and off to college. I know you can do it. I'll call all the time; I'll be home to visit." She walked over to him and laid a cool hand on his cheek. "I know you'll be alright."

She was lying, to herself and him. They both knew it, but Jake couldn't blame her. He'd have done the same thing. She had a window, a way out. She had to take it. But once she was gone, the house was unbearable.

Mary had cleaned a little, but now it stunk of liquor all the time. No one made him sandwiches or asked to read his papers. At school he made new, rougher friends, got a fake ID, and grew experienced in using it. Soon, Jake learned to take pride in how well he held his liquor. He could drink more than any of his friends but was hardly ever sick or hungover. At home, he couldn't bear to play the video games alone. Instead, he spent hour after fevered hour pounding on the keyboard, exploring the darkest corners of virtual worlds he hadn't even known existed before. He discovered that, the more he drank, the more fearless he was online. In the real world, he felt alone and nearly helpless. Online, at night, with the light from the computer screen burning in his eyes, he was powerful. He mattered. The keyboard became a weapon, and the liquor was his guide, giving him confidence to be bold, to take risks. To push further.

The programming scholarship was a gift from heaven, as sudden and unexpected as a thunderbolt. When his school counselor took him aside to tell him he had been selected, he wept. He shaved, stole money from his mom's wallet to buy new clothes, and swore to himself this was his break. He would never be like she was, would never become the wreck he saw every night when he came home. His drinking days were done. He still spent hours online, but he stopped hacking. Now he had something to lose, and he was determined not to let the chance slip away. He knew perfectly well there wouldn't be another.

For the first six weeks of freshman year, he didn't have a single drink, but there was liquor everywhere. He could smell it, and the pot, in the hallway of the dorm. His friends invited him to parties, and soon he found himself with a beer in his hand.

Then something harder.

The classes moved so quickly that he could barely keep up. All the clever tricks and bold risks he was used to taking as an anonymous hacker were useless in his carefully structured classes, and he could feel himself falling behind. He stayed up later and later, drinking more and more, desperate to keep his head above water and terrified that, no matter how hard he tried, he wouldn't be able to make it.

Just after the start of his second semester, he shot up for the first time.

He lay on the floor of his friend's dorm room and quivered in the grips of an eight-hour orgasm. When he woke, he wanted more.

After that, it all seemed to melt together, the drugs, the fights, the things he did to get money. The classes he stopped showing up for, the friends he ignored. Sometimes he sat down at the keyboard, fingers flashing as he hurried to keep up with the ideas coursing through his head. But the next day, he would realize that all the code he had written was gibberish. And his fingers shook so much it was hard to hit the keys. After a while, even his computer went untouched.

The letter telling him he had lost his scholarship lay unopened on his desk for a week. He was too high to read it.

When he had packed his bags and loaded them into his car, the only place he could go was Mary's. She had gotten pregnant and dropped out of school, but she and the guy had married, and they had an apartment now. He was working in a car shop, and she was still a secretary. They were clean and happy, and sometimes they weren't even broke.

Jake felt himself shaking the closer he got to her apartment. They had lost touch; Mary had been caught up in her new life, and he had been afraid to tell her anything real about his. He hadn't even called before heading over—he didn't know what to say. He was riding the tail end of a high, but still, he pulled over to a bar two blocks from her apartment and had a few shots to calm his nerves.

She was so happy to see him, she didn't notice the cloudiness in his eyes. She wanted him to meet the baby, only four weeks old and already louder than a brass band. Jake held the tiny infant awkwardly, gazing into its face, blinking at its bright red cheeks and flailing fists as though searching for some part of himself he had lost long ago. He didn't even feel the baby slip from his hands and wasn't sure what had happened till he heard Mary scream. She cradled the baby with all the affection she used to give to him, cried over it with the tenderness she had given him when they were kids; when she was the only one in the world who cared about him. The baby was alright, not hurt or bleeding, but when Mary wiped her tears and looked up at him, all the light had gone from her eyes.

"I love you, Jake. I always have," she said, standing in the doorway looking out at him, forlorn, on the steps. But there was no love in her voice. "But don't you *ever* come back here unless you're clean. *Totally clean.* This . . ." She looked down adoringly at the baby in her arms. "This is my life now. You can't be a part of it if you're a drunk or a junkie."

She closed the door softly, tearfully; but still, she closed it. Jake was left on the outside. He knew this was the moment: the moment of choosing. The moment that would decide the rest of his life. If he couldn't turn himself around now, he never would.

Five minutes later he was back in his car, crashing over speed-bumps, speeding toward the docks, whispering to himself, "It's okay. You'll get some soon. Just a few more minutes. It's okay . . ."

He was bouncing up and down again, but it wasn't speed-bumps now. The van was stopping, and his eyes slipped back into focus. He could hear the muffled sound of voices, and when they opened the doors, he could see an indistinct light through the blackness of the hood he wore. Fury mounted in him. Fury, confusion, and the craving that still twisted in his stomach like a knife.

"MOTHERFUCKERS!" he screamed, his voice sounding like there was gravel in his throat. He hated these men he could not see more than he had known he could hate anything. Hated them for exposing his weakness, for keeping him from what he needed most.

"Untie me!" he yelled, trying not to cry. "Untie me and see how long you stay standing! I'll *fucking* kill you!" The only response was silence and rough hands pulling at him as he bucked and thrashed uselessly. They dragged him so his chest scraped against the ground, the cement biting through his shirt and scraping his stomach till it bled. His yells became indistinct howls of rage and pain; the blood in his veins pounded like some wild drum.

Suddenly his ankles were cut free, and he was yanked to his feet. An unseen hand grabbed him roughly by the chin.

"You pretty angry now, boy?" a voice asked.

Jake didn't answer but snarled and tried to pull away.

"Alright," the voice said, satisfaction plain in every word. "I'll tell you how this is going to work. I'm gonna cut you free now and shut you in this room. Soon, very soon, somebody's going to come into this room, and that person is gonna kill you."

Jake convulsed and tried to break free, but the hands shook him violently and held him still.

"Hold still, you idiot, and listen to me. I'm going to slip a knife into your pocket, here. Feel it?" Confused, Jake froze. He nodded. "Good. Use it to kill 'em. Do that, and you go free. Do that, and I'll give you enough money to stay high on crack or heroin or whatever the hell it is you snort for the next six months. Got it?"

Jake nodded again, a small, uncertain movement, but it was enough.

"Good." the man said.

The next moment, his hands were cut free, the hood was pulled off, and he was sent sprawling through a door into a bare cement-walled room. Lying on the ground, Jake reached down to his pocket. His fingers traced the cool metal of a sharp blade. His fingers tightened around the hilt. This was something he understood, something he recognized. His mind swirled. *Just give it to me, give it to me. Anything. Anything. Anything.*

The door slammed shut, and there was nothing for Jake to do but wait.

MOLLY

Molly ran through darkness that felt oddly quiet, like the strange lack of sound that follows you to the baggage claim in the airport, when you're still waiting for your ears to pop. She felt the eerie silence from the bar like a looming presence behind her, stalking in the dark. Despite the late hour, downtown DC was still awake. People with their heads bowed against the cold hurried from coffee shops to cars while others stood, rubbing their hands together while they smoked and made off-color jokes. A homeless man, settled for the night in the doorway of a darkened shop, muttered loudly to himself as he readjusted the newspapers he had layered over his body like a blanket.

Molly streaked past them.

The sound of her feet on the pavement was a reassuring rhythm; there was something painful and familiar in the feeling of flight. She kept going, not letting her feet slow when she glanced behind her, her eyes probing the shadows. Fear had wormed into her breast, and it pulsed there, hot and painful. What had just happened? Was it something done to her, or something she had done? She wasn't sure which was the more frightening option.

She thought of Janice and Tim and the rest of the band. She had left them behind. There was something painful and familiar in that feeling, too.

She glanced behind her one more time and, seeing no one and nothing chasing her, pounded down the broken escalator steps into the metro station. Jerking her metro card over the reader, she darted into the other-worldly glimmer of the yellow lights and stood, shifting her weight from foot to foot, waiting on the platform. The gray, hole-pocked squares of faded cement that made up the metro walls stared at her with cold, empty faces. No one else stood waiting. The empty tracks faded into tunnels of impenetrable darkness. Somewhere in the distance, water dripped.

It seemed like it took hours for the train to finally come, and when it did, the roar of the train pulling up seemed out of place. The lights that flashed seemed to cry out an urgent warning that Molly could not quite understand. A crowd of people brushed by her as they stepped from the train and hurried to exit the station. An elderly lady pushing a walker, a young woman with a freshly shaved head. Molly wove through the crowd, passing by the first several cars until she found one that was empty. She stepped on and stood, not able to relax until the lights flashed and the doors closed. The train pulled out of the station and Molly threw herself into an orange plastic seat, heaving a deep breath and sliding down, so the back of her head rested against the cushion.

She pressed her fingers to her temples and closed her eyes, forcing herself to breathe, willing her heart to slow. She took a deep, rattling breath, and then another. She felt her muscles relax.

"COME," a man's voice whispered, his breath warm against her cheek.

Molly's whole body locked down, shuddering to a sudden, violent stop. She wanted to sit up, to turn around, but she couldn't. Her body was not her own—it was frozen. Her eyes slid closed as the warmth on her check coursed through her entire body, until every hair stood on end, and she shivered with pleasure reaching deep into her core.

"Come. I want you. Right now. Come to me."

There was nothing soft about that voice, nothing gentle. It was all steel and strength and command. But it was infinitely appealing. As soon as the voice stopped speaking, Molly was desperate to hear it again. To see the one who spoke.

She tried to spin around in her seat, to look behind her, but her body refused to do what she asked. The train slid into the station, lights flashed, bells rang, and the doors slid open. Finally, Molly's eyes jerked open, and she wrenched herself around, just in time to glimpse red hair and a dark form stepping out onto the platform.

She surged out of her seat, stumbling a little on feet that were suddenly heavy and clumsy. She tripped out of the metro, just seconds before the doors slammed shut, and stood dangerously close to the train as it roared back into motion. It pulled out of the station, the change in air pressure as it moved creating a wave of hot air that buffeted against her and threw her hair up into the air, streaming around her face. Even this late at night, the Chinatown station was busy. Molly stood, staring at the people that hurried past her, searching for some sign of the man whose words had had such an overpowering effect on her.

But he was gone.

I should go home. Molly told herself, her eyes still straining against the shadows that hung in the corners of the station. *I just need some sleep. I'll go home, rest, and when I wake up tomorrow, this will just feel like some crazy dream.* But in her head, her voice sounded weak and uncertain. There was another voice whispering 'come,' that drowned her voice out.

Molly knew she couldn't go home.

Instead, she started walking, keeping close to the station's gray walls, letting her fingers trail against the rough cement. She moved from one shadowy corner to the other, her breath catching in her throat and her insides twisting in panic.

She saw a dark-skinned man leaning against the station wall, partially hidden in deep shadows.

He was staring at her.

A thick curtain of dreadlocks hung down almost to his waist. His eyes burned in the darkness. This was not the same person she had encountered on the train. But Molly knew this man was waiting for her.

She walked toward him slowly. His gaze was hostile, and his eyes took her measure as she approached him. A sense of foreboding and danger mounted in her chest. She wanted to turn back, walk away, dart onto the nearest train and get away.

But her feet kept moving.

The man glowered at her. When she reached him, he stared at her for a long moment, his eyes running up and down her frame.

"He called you?" the man finally asked.

Molly nodded uncertainly.

"If you can run," he said, "this is the time to do it. I won't stop you."

Molly looked at him, shaken.

"I can't," she whispered, horrified to realize it was true. He sighed and turned, not bothering to look at her as he pulled a chain from where it had been hidden underneath his shirt, holding the key that hung from it in the palm of his hand. He ran his fingers across one gray brick, locating by touch a deep crevice in the stone. He pushed the key inside and turned it. Molly heard the click and, suddenly, a button that had been invisible a moment before glowed red just below the key. It glowed eerily in the darkness. Black letters printed on its surface read DOWN. The dreadlocked man pressed the button, and an elevator Molly hadn't realized was there sprang to life. She could hear gears shifting and cables groaning, could feel a faint shaking beneath her feet as it rose. The elevator jerked to a rest and two doors, hidden in shadow, creaked open. The man put a hand out and held them open. He turned to look at her.

Every instinct in Molly's body was telling her to run, but her feet didn't care. Her body was on automatic pilot, and no matter how loudly she screamed inside her head, her legs walked her forward. The man stepped onto the elevator behind her.

The elevator door slammed shut and everything went dark.

MOLLY

No lights inside the elevator. No buttons. No numbers that lit up as you went, accompanied by a friendly, reassuring ding. There was no mid-way stop, no between. The instant the door closed, the elevator plummeted down, down, down. Like it was being pulled by raw magnetic force to the very center of the earth, deep into some cement-walled hell that Molly had never known even existed.

It sank further than Molly could have believed possible, till her head swam and her body was sheathed in sweat from the very thought of how many crushing miles of earth must be above her. Her ears popped, and then popped again. She had never been claustrophobic, but as the moments stretched on and the elevator kept sinking, Molly felt the weight of the whole world pressing down on her.

Her lungs fought for air.

With a shudder, the elevator hit bottom, and the doors opened.

Molly stumbled out of the elevator, eager to escape the dark. Then she stood, staring around her, a sick feeling of dread twisting in her gut. She was in a corridor. A wide, empty corridor that was nothing but space and cracked, cheap linoleum. A dozen different hallways opened in every direction, each dim and vacant. Dirty light shone from bare bulbs that dangled, swaying sickly, from exposed pipes above.

The air was heavy. It sat glumly on her skin and smelled like dust. There was no fresh air down here, no wind. When the air moved, it seemed to slink from place to place lethargically; even it knew there was nowhere to go. Occasionally, the ceiling thrummed and the floors quivered as though from the bass beat of a distant song—the metro trains thundering far above them, shaking this grim world like a shuddering heartbeat.

"Quit gaping and move!" The dreadlocked man's hand clamped down on Molly's shoulder, his fingernails digging into her skin. He pushed her roughly.

At his touch, every nerve ending in Molly's body screamed in alarm. So much had happened tonight that frightened her and that she did not understand. But the rough touch against her skin was one thing she understood perfectly.

Molly spun on her heel and brought her fist sailing up to collide with the side of the man's face. Before he had even finished gasping in surprised pain, she kneed him between his legs with savage force, then shoved his spasming body to the ground. She took two steps back, keeping her eyes locked on him with laser focus and her hands up, ready to strike again, as he grabbed at himself and lay on the ground, moaning.

"I could have punched you in the throat," Molly observed coolly. "But that might have shattered your Adam's apple and killed you. I'm not sure I want to do that. Yet. But keep your hands off me, asshole. No one shoves me around. Not ever."

"You God-damned little whore," the man groaned as he climbed slowly to his feet. Molly shifted her weight from one foot to the other. If he lunged at her, she decided, she'd go for his kneecaps first.

He braced his hands against his knees and stood, hunched over with pain, breathing hard. "You have no fucking idea who I am, or what I can do to you," he looked up, his eyes burning through the black curtain of his hair. "But you'll find out soon enough."

Molly braced for his attack, her whole body vibrating with tension, like a guitar string pulled too tight. But the man didn't reach out for her or even step in her direction.

He hummed.

At first, Molly didn't understand what was happening. She narrowed her eyes and shuffled her feet, still expecting the man to throw himself at her. Then the sound emanating from him changed. The humming grew louder. The man pulled his lips back from his teeth and hissed.

Molly felt her knees lock.

The sound throbbed in her ears. Her head pounded, her toes and fingers tingled painfully. Molly opened her mouth and realized that she couldn't get enough air in to fill her lungs. She tried to move her hands, but her arms were frozen, useless, at her sides. She felt her eyes widen as she stared at the man in confused horror.

He smirked and stepped toward her.

"Tyler!" a voice boomed from behind her. "What the hell is going on?"

As suddenly as it had started, the hissing sound stopped. As soon as the sound faded from her ears, Molly's knees unlocked, and her lungs expanded. She staggered, lightheaded, and leaned heavily against the wall to keep herself from falling over.

Tyler's eyes focused just over Molly's shoulder, and she saw a flash of fear in his eyes he quickly covered over with a sneer.

"She punched me in the face!" he answered, his tone reminding Molly of a preschooler tattle-telling on the playground. She wanted to turn and see who was coming up behind her, but she knew better than to turn her back on Tyler's still-hostile expression.

"Calm down," the booming voice ordered. "She's been through a lot, and she has no idea who you are. You can't blame her for defending herself." He reached Molly's side, and she could finally see him. Blue eyes and red hair. A slender face edged in scarlet stubble that gave him a slightly unkempt look. The loose, slightly curly locks of his red hair fell around his face in casual disarray. The white button-down shirt that he wore over jeans fit him loosely, and hung, untucked, around his hips.

"Molly," he said, his voice warm as coffee, the sound of it making the muscles in her stomach unclench just a little. "Welcome. I'm so glad we found you in time." He reached out and folded her hand in both of his. "I'm sorry if Tyler upset you. His social skills sometimes fall a little short, but I promise—we're here to help you."

"I remember you," Molly pulled her hand away and stepped back, angling her body so she could keep both men in her line of sight. She desperately wished she knew why she had come here in the first place, and how to get out. "You were in the bar tonight. Watching me." She might not have noticed him, if not for the flame-red hair that framed his face in loose curls. The brief glimpse she had had of him burned in her mind, as did the memory of the smile that had creased his face when everyone else in the bar stood frozen and stared hungrily at her.

"I was. Luckily for all of us. I'm Andrew. We've got a lot to talk about. Come. We'll go somewhere more comfortable, and I'll answer as many of your questions as I can."

"What is this place?" Molly had to fight not to take another step away. She practically had her back up against the wall already.

Andrew spread out his hands. "This is the Refuge. It's a place where people like us can be safe."

"People like us?"

"Yes. You might not realize it yet, Molly, but you are in way, way over your head. I am very grateful I was there tonight so that, after what happened, I could get to you first. We were very, very lucky."

"Lucky?" Her throat felt dry, and her voice scratched. "Why am I lucky?"

"Because the chances are good that, if I hadn't found you tonight, by now you would already be dead."

Molly felt a sharp wave of shock.

"It's a lot to take in, I know." Andrew stepped closer but didn't try to touch her again. Molly appreciated that. "I'm sure you have a million questions, and I promise, I will do my best to answer as many of them as I can. But let's go inside, alright? We can sit down and talk. Even if we talk till the sun comes up, down here it won't make much of a difference." He smiled at her then; a broad smile that warmed his eyes.

"Alright," she nodded. "I'll come with you and talk."

"Right this way." He held out an arm and motioned further down the hallway, and kept pace with her as she walked.

"Is everything else ready, Tyler?" he called out over his shoulder.

"Yes, sir," Tyler replied quickly. "We caught a fresh one earlier tonight, just like you wanted. We're all set."

"Great. Why don't you start getting everyone together? We'll meet you there in a bit."

Until this point, Molly had been so focused on trying to figure out what the hell was going on that she had noticed little about her physical surroundings. All she knew was that the elevator had taken her further down into the earth than she ever wanted to be and she had come out of the elevator into a plain, poorly lit hallway.

Now Andrew came to a halt in front of an iron door so tall that Molly had to tip her head back to see the top. Several thick, gleaming rods of metal crisscrossed the door, sinking deep into the wall on either side and even into the floor and to the ceiling. The rods were connected to complex gears, all linked to a round handle that sat in the center of the board next to a small, copper keyhole. The corner of Andrew's mouth twisted into a smile when he saw her gaping at it.

"We pilfer as much electricity from the metro system as we dare," he explained, as he pulled out a key that hung from a chain around his neck and unlocked the door. "But we use all of it to run our ventilation. It takes a lot of electricity to keep the air down here breathable. We can't take any more power than we do now without getting noticed. We've already been the cause of two fare increases. If we were responsible for prices going up even more, someone would be sure to get so angry that they'd figure out the truth. So, we get a little bit creative." He turned the key, and the corridor filled with the sound of scraping metal. The rods retracted, the door swung open slowly, and warm red light, the color of the sunrise, spilled out, filling the dark corridor with a ruby red glow. "Ah. Here we go." Andrew tucked his key back under his shirt, stepped through the door, and reached out a hand to help Molly up over the step. "Welcome home."

MOLLY

Molly stared through the doorway. In her gut, she knew that if she stepped through it, her life would change forever.

Andrew was wrong. This wasn't her home. Molly knew what her life was; she had fought and clawed and worked her butt off to create it. Her life was back on the surface, in the bar, with a microphone in her hands and her band beside her. This was just some bad dream, a twisted trip down a rabbit's hole, into some alternate universe where she did not belong.

But Andrew said she was in danger. And things had happened to her tonight she didn't understand. Molly wanted her life back, but she couldn't just walk back into the bar and get back onto the stage. She had to figure it out what had happened to her, so she could make sure that it never, ever happened again. Besides, she had the distinct feeling that neither Tyler or Andrew would just let her get back on that elevator and wander away. She wouldn't have minded taking them on in a physical fight. But it was clear they had some weird abilities that would make sure any fight she had with them would not be physical.

She took a deep breath. She would figure this shit out. She

would get back what was hers. The answers she needed were on the other side of that metal door.

Molly squared her shoulders, ignored Andrew's outstretched hand, and stepped over the threshold to the other side.

It was like stepping into an alternate universe. The dark shadows and plain, rough cement walls were gone, replaced with walls covered in a smooth, shiny substance that gleamed like copper. She stood in a hallway so wide that she instantly guessed it must have once, a long time ago, been a subway tunnel. Light shone from lanterns spaced out every few feet, flooding the chamber with a warm, rosy light. Molly wondered if they were gas lanterns, burning with real flames, but the heavy tint of the glass made it hard to tell. The ceiling was covered with exposed bronze pipes of various sizes and thicknesses, and intricately patterned tiles glittered under her feet.

"Right this way," Andrew murmured, and led Molly around a corner.

Molly followed, and almost crashed head-first into the girl standing right beside an oval door. Standing with a backpack slung over one shoulder, and a strained expression on her face, the girl from the bar looked up at Molly with a tight smile. "I guess my warning didn't help much, did it?" she said, then her eyes hardened as Andrew came around the corner.

"Tyler said you wanted to see me," she told him.

"Evie," Andrew's face fell. "I think you already know what I'm going to say."

The girl lifted her chin but said nothing.

"I built this place to be a Refuge for Echoes. You are not one of us. But when you came to me, I took you in anyway. I arranged for you to get into the school you wanted. I paid for you to get new, forged ID. I've done everything I can for you. But my responsibility is to people like Molly. The reality we are living in right now is a harsh one. The people I protect are being hunted down, one by one. We can't afford mistakes, and we can't afford defiance. I made that very clear to you when I took you in."

"I've helped you," Evie protested fiercely, her eyes flashing. "I've done months and months of research for you, gotten you all the information you wanted."

"That research has only led to dead-ends," Andrew exclaimed, frustration leaking into his tone. "And you are working against me, and putting my own people at risk. You haven't left me any choice. I have to rescind my offer of safe haven."

As soon as the words left his mouth, all the defiance disappeared from Evie's face. "You . . . you can't mean that," she whispered, a tremor in her voice.

"You'll be alright." Andrew put a hand on her shoulder. "You can keep your ID. Keep your enrollment in your classes. The car I bought you . . . everything. But you can't come back here."

"But Andrew . . ." Evie's eyes were round and shone with fear. "They'll find me. You know they will."

Andrew shook his head sharply. "I don't believe that for a second. You're a smart girl. I've been where you are now, Evie. Only I was a lot younger than you, and I didn't have any resources at all. I know it can be done. Just keep up your studies, and keep your head down. But this isn't the place for you anymore."

"This is because I told you that you were wrong about the goblet," Evie cried, her cheeks flushing. "I want things to change just as much as you do, Andrew. You know that. But what you're trying to do now is a mistake."

"We've had our disagreements, but this decision is about safety. For my people, and ultimately for you, too." He stepped closer to her and lowered his voice, but Molly could still hear him. "You know that you take a risk every time you come here," he whispered. Evie dropped her eyes. "You are surrounded by people with an amazing ability, that you have no way to resist. I've tried to make sure that no one here . . . takes advantage. But I can't watch over you all the time. This is the best thing, for everyone."

Evie didn't say anything. Molly thought she saw moisture gathering in the girl's eyes.

"I have to ask you to return the key I gave you," Andrew said, holding out his hand.

Evie's eyes shone with unshed tears as she pulled off the key hanging around her neck. Slowly, she placed it in Andrew's palm. His fingers closed over it, and for a second they stared at each other. Evie stepped back, as though afraid to turn her back on him.

"You're making a mistake," she whispered. "Deep down, I think you know that."

"Good luck," Andrew said, his voice ringing with finality. Evie spun on her heel and fled down the hallway.

For a second Andrew stared after her. When she was gone, he closed his eyes and rubbed his forehead.

"I never should have let her come here," he said, to himself as much as to Molly. He opened his eyes and looked over at Molly. "You must think I'm a terrible person," he said. "I don't blame you. But you haven't seen the things I've seen. You don't know how hard we have to work to keep hidden, to stay safe. How important the work I do is. There are harsh realities we can't afford to ignore."

With a shake of his head, he turned to the oval door with a small round window at the top. It looked like it ought to be on a submarine somewhere, and he unlocked it with another key pulled from a chain around his neck. Turning the circular handle with a practiced flourish, he swung the door open and stood aside to let her enter.

The spacious room held several thick leather chairs and a broad desk of mahogany wood. A fire burned in the small fireplace, filling the room with flickering shadows and the smell of wood smoke.

"Are you cold?" Andrew asked, motioning toward the fire as

she held her fingers out toward the flame. "Feel free to warm up. It can get a bit nippy down here."

"I'm fine." It wasn't true; Molly's skin was covered in goosebumps, and she still wished for her leather jacket, but she didn't want to tell Andrew that, or to huddle in front of his fire. Instead, she crossed her arms over her chest.

"These are my living quarters," Andrew motioned around, either not noticing her discomfort or tactfully ignoring it. "Let me get you something hot to drink, and then we can sit down and chat. Hang on a second." Before Molly could respond, he turned and hurried away. She took the opportunity to walk around the room, trying to take in everything. There were no windows, but two walls were covered with huge floor to ceiling maps drawn in stark black and white. One map was of all of Washington DC, the others of an area she couldn't identify, but seemed to be right near the ocean. This map was covered with push pins and had been drawn on extensively. Red circles dotted the map's surface like an erupting rash, and notes in a nearly illegible hand were scribbled thickly around the corners. The one bare wall had been covered almost ceiling to floor with charts, and more maps. The wall was practically papered with hand-drawn sketches of a goblet or cup. Andrew strode back into the room, two steaming mugs of coffee in his hands, and Molly turned away from the drawings. He sat down at the small table in the center of the room, setting one cup in front of himself and the other out in front of the empty chair.

"Join me," he invited her. Molly lowered herself onto the empty chair, perching on the edge. She didn't pick up the cup of coffee Andrew set out for her.

"So," she said, folding her hands tightly in her lap, "why don't you tell me what's going on? You said this place is called the Refuge. A refuge from what? And what did you mean that I'd be dead by now if I hadn't come down here?"

"I meant just what I said." Andrew put down his coffee cup and shook his head. "What you did tonight at the bar was impressive—

I'll give you that. But it was also extremely risky. Declaring your power publicly like that just makes you a target."

"Listen, Andrew," Molly leaned forward, "maybe you haven't caught onto this yet, but I have no idea what you're talking about. I need some actual answers, asap. All I know right now is that tonight at the bar everybody, including my best friends, suddenly did their best zombie impressions. And then, apparently, you followed me onto the metro and did something. What *did* you do on the train, anyway? When I try to remember it, my brain goes kind of fuzzy."

"I did the same thing to you that you did to all those people in the bar," Andrew answered, speaking as though he was stating the obvious. "I used the power of my voice to force you to do what I told you to do."

"What does that even mean?" Molly cried, fighting the sudden urge to rip out her hair, or knock Andrew to the ground and strangle him until he actually said something comprehensible. "None of this makes any sense! I didn't do anything to those people in the bar. Really!" she cried, seeing the disbelief in Andrew's eyes. "I was just singing. I mean, I remember the words kind of burning in my throat. And then the band stopped playing, and everyone was staring at me, and . . ."

Andrew's expression morphed into shock as her words faltered.

"You . . . you can't actually be serious," he stammered. "You've been on our radar for a while now as a Potential. I assumed that you knew what you were doing but just didn't understand the risks you were taking. And then, after what you did tonight, we needed to act quickly."

"But I don't know what I did!" Molly closed her eyes, her hands closing into fists on the table top as she struggled to get her frustration under control. "If I did do. . . something . . . it was a total accident. I need to understand it so that I can make sure it never happens again. That's all I want—honestly, I just want to go back to my life.

She looked up at Andrew. His eyes were wide.

"Shit," Andrew whispered, staring down at the table top with a dazed expression. "This is fucking amazing."

He sprang to his feet and paced. "I had no idea," he said, running a hand through his hair. "I mean, I could hear how powerful your voice was. But I assumed that you were doing it on purpose. Showing off for fun, not realizing that you were putting yourself at risk. But if you threw a loop around that whole room . . . over a hundred freaking people . . . without knowing what you were doing? I've never seen anything like that before. This could change everything," he whispered, almost to himself. Then he turned and hurried over to sit back down across from Molly.

"I owe you an apology," he said, leaning in toward her anxiously. "I misread this situation. You have to understand that, genetically, even though being an Echo is a recessive trait . . . it does run in families. Most people grow up hearing stories. Rumors. Enough so if it starts to happen to them, they at least know what is happening. Some of them even know enough to know what their new 'gift' might cost them."

Molly shrugged. She had no idea what rumors might be running around her family, and it wasn't like she was going to call home and ask. Andrew was still talking, and Molly shook herself and re-focused on his words.

"Every once in a while, we do find someone who really has no clue about their heritage and what's happening to them. But they're using their voices by accident, it's always minor stuff. They'll manage to talk their way out of a parking ticket, or maybe they get a great deal on a new car. But nothing like what you did. It never occurred to me that you could be wielding power like that unintentionally. Even with years of training and practice, I don't think there are more than three people here who can do what you did last night. And if you did that without even knowing what you are . . ." Andrew sat back slowly in his chair. "You might be the strongest Echo we've had."

"Okay," Molly held up her hands, trying to stem the tide of overwhelming information. "Hold on. First of all, what do you mean 'knowing what I am'?"

Andrew hesitated. "I'm not sure how to explain this, Molly. Have you ever heard of the Sirens?"

"I guess?" Molly answered, hazy memories of high school English class swirling somewhere deep in her mind. "They're birds, right? The Greeks wrote about them."

Andrew grimaced. "Well, the Greeks got almost everything wrong. Their myths describe half-bird women who lived by the sea and use their hypnotic voices to lure sailors to their death. The truth is a lot worse than that. Vampires, demons, every horror story you've ever heard, at its core, has been about them. They're monsters." Andrew shuddered, and Molly felt her own skin prickle. "A long time ago, the Sirens—or, as we call them, Watchers—mixed with humans and had some half-blood children. For people like us, those genes were hidden down deep, somewhere in the family tree. When they do finally express themselves, you get us. The Echoes. Our power is like a distant echo of the more powerful abilities of our somewhat questionable forbearers."

"So, you're saying that I'm, what . . . descended from the Sirens?" Molly asked, rubbing her temples. It all sounded so ridiculous.

"Very distantly related, yes," Andrew nodded. "And the distance is why we look human—and why our voices are so much weaker than theirs. Compared to them, our power is almost nothing. When we throw a loop around someone, most of the time it only lasts a few minutes. Once you hear a Siren's voice, their power over you lasts forever." The tenor of Andrew's voice changed, and something was defiant in his tone. "The Watchers are still around, which is one reason that we have to stay hidden.

The Legacies are the other. But we deserve better than to be forced to live in hiding, and we're going to change all of that. And now that you're here . . ." Andrew's eyes glowed with determination. "The Watcher's time is almost over. Then the Legacies will be forced to admit that we're a legitimate power. They'll be forced to stop hunting us, and will join with us instead."

"Wait, who are the Legacies? There are *other* people hunting me now?" Molly cried, incredulous.

"You're safe here. Don't worry." Andrew stood up, pushing his hair behind his ears and reaching out a hand. This time, Molly took it. "The Refuge is a secret that they don't even know exists. We work very hard to keep it that way. And the best thing we can do for you is to get you fully integrated here as quickly as possible."

"I don't want to be integrated here," Molly interjected. "All I want is to get a handle on this situation so that I can go back to my real life."

Andrew nodded distractedly. "Everyone should be gathered by now. We should get going. We can talk more once the initiation is done."

Molly stopped short. "What are you talking about?" She demanded. "I didn't agree to go through any kind of initiation."

"It's for your own good," Andrew said, raising his hands defensively when he saw the flash of indignation on her face. "And yes, I know exactly how that sounds. But here's the thing, Molly. We've been building this community for years. And we've found that, often, in order for a person's voice to fully express itself, we have to bring it to the surface. That means for your voice to reach its full potential, we have to force it out. Think of it in terms of a mother bird pushing its fledgling out of the nest. Yes, it's harsh. I'm not going to pretend that it isn't. Believe me, if I thought there was another way, I'd be the first to pursue it. But it isn't safe to be one of us if you don't have control of your abilities. Your abilities are what keep you safe."

"No," Molly said shaking her head vigorously and stepping back. "I won't do it. You haven't been listening to me, Andrew. I don't belong here. I don't want any of this."

Andrew stepped closer and laid a gentle hand on her shoulder.

"I'm sorry," he said, "but I have a responsibility to keep you safe. I've seen what can happen to Echoes who make the wrong choice. *You will go through the initiation.*" His voice dropped, his words drew out, longer and longer, the sound of them rippling through the air, making Molly's head ring painfully. "You *will* become one of us." His voice swelled, slamming against Molly's will like an unforgiving wave. Her body jerked, as though she had been punched in the stomach. She lurched forward, grabbing the table for support as her legs went weak and a wave of dizziness hit her hard. She pulled in air convulsively.

"What did you just do to me?" she gasped, though her chest felt tight and her eyes were blurry.

"There's a reason that I'm in charge here," Andrew explained. He stuck his hands deep in his pockets and looked away from her, as though he couldn't quite bear to look her in the eyes. "I've defeated every single Echo in this place with my voice. Some of them more than once, if they didn't get the full picture the first time. Listen, I don't blame you for being angry with me, Molly. I know this is all happening fast, and I don't expect you to accept everything I'm telling you after just a few minutes of conversations. But I know—even if you don't yet—what we're up against. I know what could happen to you up there." He grimaced and looked down at the floor. "I can't lose any more people to those monsters. I won't let it happen. I'll do whatever I have to do to keep us safe." He nodded to himself and straightened up. "We should go." He opened the door and held it open for her.

Molly tried to keep her feet from moving. She tried to dig in her heels, throw back her head, and refuse. But her feet were on automatic pilot. They did what Andrew wanted without ever checking in with her brain or her heart. Molly ground her teeth together in frustration as she walked with Andrew through the hallway. But there was nothing she could do to stop.

A crowd waited for them in front of a large set of metal double doors. Molly tried to take in the faces, but there were too many, and her worry over what was about to happen had reached a fever pitch, making it hard for her to do anything but try wildly to think of a way to escape. The crowd surged around her, closing her in. She could hear people whispering. She saw a young blonde-haired woman, about her age, peering at her with worried eyes. Tyler strode forward to meet them as they approached.

"We're all ready here, Tyler?" Andrew asked brusquely. Tyler nodded.

Andrew turned to Molly, his eyes harder than she remembered them being just a moment before.

"You're going to go into the room now," he explained, "and you must go in alone. Inside this room, there is a man and fire. The man doesn't matter. He's just a bum that we pulled off the streets. The thing that matters about him is that he has never been broken to the voice. His will is untouched. To earn your place among us, you must master your abilities enough to overcome his most powerful instinct . . . the instinct for self-preservation. To pass this test, you must command the man to put his hand into the fire. And he must obey you."

"What?" Molly cried in horror. "You're out of your mind. I'm not doing that! Wait a minute . . . Andrew!"

But Andrew stepped away, and suddenly Tyler was behind her, pulling her arms together and binding her wrists. Molly kicked and cursed and tried to pull away. But in an instant, Tyler had opened the door and shoved her through. The door slammed shut behind her; Molly heard a key turn in the lock.

She stood frozen, and blinked in the darkness. Orange flames danced in a small fire pit in the center of the room, casting strange, flickering shadows all around. The room was empty and bare, save for the form that stood hunched by the fire. Panic surged in her chest as the man turned toward her.

Then the firelight splashed against his face.

"Jake?" Molly cried, unbelieving. She felt a moment of hope . . . almost happiness, at the sight of him. "Is that you?"

He looked up at her, but there was no recognition in his eyes. There was only desperation and fury.

The next second, he was yelling, running toward her, his raised knife aimed directly at her heart.

EVIE

Evie stood outside the metro station. She couldn't stop trembling.

I have nowhere to go.

Going to the bar had been a mistake. What had she been thinking? What made her believe she could succeed in getting between Andrew and something—or someone—that he wanted? She hadn't realized he would be at the bar tonight. She had hoped she could convince Molly to disappear without anyone else knowing, and before it was too late for all of them.

No, she told herself firmly, *don't think like that. It isn't too late. I helped create this situation, and I can still put things right.* Her fingers closed around the USB key that hung from a string around her neck, underneath the moon necklace she always wore. When Andrew had asked for her door key, she had been terrified that he would ask for the USB, too. She wouldn't have been able to refuse him. She wasn't sure if he hadn't thought of it, or if it just hadn't occurred to him that leaving her with all the results of their research might be a danger to his plans. After all, he had found what he wanted. And what threat could she, a young college student without the slightest shred of power, be to him? Evie adjusted the weight of the backpack on her shoulders and pulled her hoodie over her face. The shadows on the ground around her wavered and stirred like living things. Her breath made ghostly puffs in the frigid air, and the slightest slice of sunrise stained the sky with pink and gray.

She took a deep breath and closed her eyes. Her heart was still racing, but she could feel the first surge of panic wearing off. *Ok,* she told herself. *This is bad. I will not pretend that it isn't. But I've been in worse situations.* Memory threatened to sweep her away, and she flinched and forced the old images away with a shudder. ***Much*** *worse situations. It might be true that, right now, I've got no place to sleep, no one to protect me, and no money for food. But I am* ***not*** *helpless. Andrew has no idea who he's dealing with. He was a fool to let me walk away.*

Part of it, she suspected, was that he'd never even bothered to read all the information she had brought to him. And he'd never suspected there was a good deal of her research that she'd never brought to him.

Her first plan had been warning Molly, and that had backfired spectacularly. But she had another plan. A plan flitted around the edges of her mind for weeks, whispering to her at night, right before she fell asleep. A desperate, risky, wildly impractical plan that now, standing in the first rays of dirty sunlight, suddenly seemed like the most obvious, natural thing in the world. There were still a few pieces missing, but she could fix that . . . all she needed was some time.

Her cell phone vibrated, and Evie started violently before shaking herself and digging her phone out of her back pocket. She didn't have to check the phone to see who was calling—there was only one person it could be.

"Hey, Bea! Are you okay?"

"Sure. More or less." Bea's voice was raspy and uneven. "I just wanted to . . . shit, is that the time? Is it really only 5:00 a.m.? I'm sorry Evie. Chemo brain is the worst. I thought it was later than that. I didn't mean to wake you."

"Don't worry about it—I was up anyway. How are you feeling?" Evie cringed as the words left her lips, knowing it was the wrong thing to ask. She knew the answer already, and asking would just make Bea feel obliged to lie.

"Better, thanks," Bea fibbed, just as Evie had known she would. "I had a favor to ask, but I can call back at a decent hour."

"No, don't bother. What can I do?"

"I need a ride," Bea said, frustration plain in her voice. "I'm not supposed to drive right now, not with all the stuff I'm on. But I've got an appointment tomorrow. It's kind of a big one and . . . well, the thing is, I don't want folks there. I need to talk to the doctor without them around. So . . . could you take me?"

"Are you kidding? Of course!" Evie's heart twisted. She had felt so helpless ever since Bea got sick. She was so happy to have something she could actually do to be helpful.

"You're the best, Evie. Thanks. I'll text you later with the time —I can't even remember when the freaking appointment is right now. But are you okay? Your voice sounds . . . kind of strained. Did something happen?"

For a heady second, Evie imagined telling her friend the truth. Imagined how good it would feel to answer honestly, to talk to someone she trusted, who could help her think through what to do. Someone who would just listen. But the surge of excitement faded almost instantaneously. Evie thought of her friend, of the surgeries, the medications, and shame made her throat tight. How could she add her problems to all the burdens Bea was already carrying? As far as Bea knew, Evie was just a regular college student, and it had to stay that way. The last thing Evie wanted was to somehow draw Bea into the dangers she was facing. If she were less selfish, she would cut off all interactions with her friend for Bea's safety. Evie wasn't strong enough to do that, but she could at least shield her friend as well as she was able.

"No, I'm fine. Just sleepy. That's all."

"Long night last night, huh? Are you gonna skip class?" Bea's voice took on a familiar, teasing ring. "You know you can if you want to, right?"

Class! Evie bit her lip. She had forgotten all about class and school. But now that she stopped to think about it, class ought to be the first thing on her mind. For ten months, she had stayed hidden. Now more than ever, it was important for her to keep up her routine, to preserve the cover that Andrew had constructed for her.

"No, I'll go. Do you still want me to send you my notes from class?"

"Don't bother." Bea tried to sound casual, but Evie could hear the bitterness in her voice. "I'm not coming back to school this semester. That was just a fairy tale the doctors told my parents to try to keep them from losing their minds completely. But I'll see you tomorrow, okay? Sorry again for calling you so early."

"Don't worry about it! See you soon."

Having Bea's voice in her ear had made her feel a little better, but after she hung up, Evie felt even more alone. She checked her watch. The first trains of the day would be running any minute. She had to be smart now. Her car was parked by campus, miles away. The last thing in the world she wanted was to walk back down into the shadowy metro center, to put herself anywhere near Andrew or his minions. But she didn't have a choice. She wrapped her hands around her backpack straps, the weight on her back a familiar comfort. Then she squared her shoulders and walked back into the station.

EVIE

Evie was the first person on the train; she had never seen it so spotless. She sat stiff-backed and rim-rod straight, her eyes raking the face of every new person who boarded the car. Morning rush hour swelled around her, and the tension inside her built with every face she scanned. She wasn't sure what she was looking for. But she was frightened.

When she finally climbed out of the station and made it to campus, she let out a shaky sigh of relief and hurried to the lecture hall. The janitors had already unlocked the doors, and she slipped inside, grateful for the warmth, for the shelter, for the chance she might rest a little before class. She leaned her head back and closed her eyes, though there was no way she could sleep with her body still so full of tension.

When other students filed in, Evie did her best to ignore them—especially the girl two seats down from her, who was eating a bagel. Evie tried not to watch. It smelled good, though, which made it harder. It wasn't like Evie had never been hungry before, but now the hunger had a new, raw edge of panic to it. Now she didn't know where her next meal would come from or if it would come at all.

She knew there must be an office on campus, somewhere she could ask for help finding food, and a place to live. But they would ask questions. Look at her file. Maybe notice that her transcripts were forged and her IDs faked. Panic made her chest tight. Evie shook her head and sank lower into her seat. She couldn't ask for help. She'd have to figure something out, though. Soon.

Her phone buzzed in her pocket, and she pulled it out.

"Hey Evie," Bea's message read. *"Almost forgot to tell you happy birthday!"*

Evie groaned inwardly. Until this moment, she had kept from remembering herself.

"Thanks," she texted back, glad that Bea wouldn't be able to see her pained expression through the phone. Then she shook herself. It didn't matter she was hungry, or that today she was turning twenty-one and had never felt more alone in her life. For the moment, she was safe. She was free. She was a straight A student. That would have to be enough.

"Are those creepy hot guys there yet?" Bea asked, and Evie rolled her eyes.

"They are not creepy," she insisted, tapping out the words forcefully. It felt good to talk to Bea. It was such a nice break from the panic. *"Don't be a jerk."*

"Can't help it. It comes so naturally to me." Evie pictured Bea smirking with a glint of humor dancing in her eye. *"They are creepy. Non-creepy people do not wear heavy leather trench coats all the time. The big one is always practically drooling over you."*

"I'm the only one in this whole class, other than his brother, that he can talk to without using his interpreter." Evie insisted, blushing a little. *"You can't blame him for wanting to chat."*

"Oh, he wants more than a chat, sweetheart. Believe me."

Evie laughed out loud, looking up just in time to see the two brothers, who were signing animatedly to each other, walk into the room. Their interpreter took his seat next to the podium at the front of the room while the brothers settled down in chairs just in front of him.

"They're here now." Evie updated Bea.

"Cool. Tell me what they're saying."

"Not sure." Evie tried not to stare openly. *"When they're just signing to each other, they don't use American sign. They're using some other sign language. Probably one from the country they were born in. They only use ASL when they're talking to their interpreter. Besides, it isn't nice to eavesdrop."*

"Are you kidding me? What's the fun in knowing another language if you can't even eavesdrop on people?!"

Evie smiled and looked back over at the brothers. She wondered what country they were from originally. But even when she couldn't understand, Evie loved to watch. The taller brother was signing now, and it took her breath away, the way his powerful fingers could move so swiftly, the way his whole upper body moved fluidly despite his thick build, becoming a part of whatever he was saying. Even through the sleeves of his long leather jacket, she could see the outline of muscles twisting down his arms. His thick eyebrows were pulled together now, his flawless face dark as he leaned in toward his slender, blonde-haired brother. It looked like they were arguing.

That seemed to happen a lot.

"Class is starting. I gotta go," she texted Bea.

"Sure. Wouldn't want to risk distracting you and having your GPA slip to a 3.98. That would be a disaster." Bea added in a smiley face sticking out its tongue. *"Ttyl."*

Evie texted back her own smiley face with its tongue sticking out, and then tucked her phone away.

The lecture started, and Evie paid close attention to both the interpreter and the professor. Every time she saw the interpreter use a sign she didn't know, she jotted down a note in the margins of her paper. At the beginning of the year, there had been two interpreters. She had especially liked watching the woman, who wore high heels and stylish suits, with her hair always looking like she had just stepped out of a salon. But she had stopped coming a few weeks ago, and now the male interpreter had to do the whole two-hour lecture by himself. She pitied him, wondering how he kept going for so long, admiring the way he took the professor's words and drew them precisely in the air, reconstructing them as a perfect, visual whole.

The lecture ended, and Evie closed her notebook, standing as she pulled her backpack out from under her chair. She tried not to look up, to see if he was coming over, and instead focused on gathering her things. When she felt a not-quite-familiar tap on her shoulder, she jumped, and her notebook spilled from her hands onto the floor.

"I'm so sorry," Roman signed, his warm, brown eyes wide. *"I didn't mean to startle you. I just wanted to say hello."*

"No, it's not your fault. I'm on edge today," Evie signed back. She reached down to retrieve her notebook, but Roman beat her to it. His eyes drifted down to the page as he reached out to hand it back, at the page crowded with the deliberate, cramped curves of her notes.

"W-O-W" he signed, his fingers jumping as he spelled the word out. *"You've taken a lot of notes. Is this whole notebook just for this one class?"*

"It's my second notebook for this class, actually," Evie admitted, wincing a little. She hated looking like a nerd, but it was hard to hide it.

"Really?" Roman's face grew thoughtful. *"Would you be willing to let me make photocopies of these? It's hard for me to take notes when I have to always be watching the interpreter, and it would be really helpful. I'm having such a difficult time in this class."* He turned his back so that only she could see what he was signing. *"My poor interpreter thinks I'm failing because of the language barrier. The truth is, it's too much detail for me. I can't keep all these names and dates straight in my head."*

"Oh, sure, that's no problem," Evie answered, wishing she had thought to offer earlier. *"Actually, I had been planning to share my notes with someone who isn't going to end up needing them. I'd be happy to share them with you instead."*

"Thanks," Roman signed, and his eyes lit up, leaving her nearly speechless. *"Are you busy now? We could walk right over to the library and make copies."*

"Um, I guess I'm not," Evie's fingers tripped over the words, and she could feel the heat rising in her cheeks. *"I mean, yes. Um. I . . . I don't really have anywhere I need to be. Right now, that is."*

"Perfect!" Roman grinned. *"Hold on a second, let me just go tell my brother."*

"Get a grip!" Evie muttered to herself, as she turned to shove her notebook, a little more forcefully than necessary, into her bag. "This isn't a big deal. Other students chat with each other all the time. Regular people don't feel lightheaded because of two minutes of conversation and the idea of going to the library with a boy." Resolutely, Evie pulled the zipper of her bag shut. It was only when she looked up that she realized they were arguing.

Roman and his brother were again conversing in a dialect of sign she didn't understand, but she knew from their facial expressions, from the way their hands flew, both signing as though they were trying to drown each other out. The interpreter stood off to the side, hands folded in front of him. Watching. Roman's brother, the slender one with long blond hair, kept glancing in her direction and gesturing toward her. He was shaking his head and looked furious.

They argued for several minutes while Evie watched, transfixed. A few times she saw a sign she thought she recognized, but she understood no more than that. The younger brother's face grew flushed, and his signs got bigger, his hands cutting through the air. Suddenly Roman stepped toward his brother and, for a split second, Evie thought he would strike him. His chest expanded, and he seemed to grow taller, wider. His eyes flashed dangerously. Evie saw the interpreter take a hasty step away.

There was a moment when everything seemed frozen. Then the younger brother dropped his head. His shoulders fell, and he looked down at the floor. Evie felt a tingle run down her spine as she watched Roman glower at him for a moment, as though watching to make sure his brother made no further protest. Then he turned, spinning on his heel, and strode over to her. All the fierceness melted out of him in an instant.

"Who knew that going to school with my younger brother would be like having my mother follow me around from class to class?" He rolled his eyes. *"I hate it when people try to tell me what to do."*

She smiled back, though deep down, she felt a pang of uneasiness. *"I know exactly what you mean. I like my independence, too."* Roman lay his hand on her shoulder and gently guided her from the room. Evie only dimly knew of Roman's brother, standing with arms folded, watching as they passed through the doors.

"I was noticing your necklace. I like it," Roman said, as they walked across campus.

The small, stone-white circle, was carefully crafted so you could see the gray shadows on its face. Evie smiled and rubbed it affectionately between her fingers. There was a groove there, right where she always touched it.

"Thanks," she signed. *"It's the moon. It keeps me safe."*

Roman glanced at her sharply but made no comment.

The library was bright, warm, and nearly empty—just how Evie liked it. It didn't take long to make the copies, and Roman paid for them without making any comment, for which Evie was grateful. She settled down in her favorite spot and read, and Roman brought back her notebook when he was done.

"This is going to help me so much." He hefted the thick sheaf of papers in his hand, measuring its weight. *"Thank you. I may even have a chance of passing the test on Thursday."* He hesitated. *"You*

wouldn't want to study together for a while, would you? I don't want to be a bother, but I don't have any classes this afternoon."

Evie hesitated. The USB key felt heavy around her neck, and her fingers itched to get back to her research. But it had been a long time since she had just sat and chatted with anyone. Even Bea, who could always make Evie smile, had been so sick she hadn't been able to spend much time socializing in months. Besides, Evie told herself, I have to act like a typical college student. Before she could stop herself, her eyes ran up and down Roman's impressive frame. There wasn't any doubt in her mind what a normal college student would do. *"Sure!"* she signed cheerfully and set aside her book.

Two hours later, they had yet to do much actual studying.

Evie was laughing. A real laugh—a laugh so deep her stomach hurt and her eyes filled with tears. It felt like a miracle, to have tears that weren't shed out of fear or heartbreak tumble down her checks. The laughter, she thought, gazing at Roman sitting across the table from her, was as good as a birthday present. She kept reminding herself that they were in a library, and she honestly tried to keep quiet. But it had been a long, long time since Evie laughed. Now she just couldn't seem to hold the sound inside.

Roman laughed with her, still moving his hands precisely in the air, telling her the story of his first day at school, of how lost he had gotten, and his disastrous attempt to, through gestures, get directions from a passing student while his brother hopped from foot to foot, close to having a fit because they were so late.

It wasn't fluid; there were some signs he used that weren't ASL, and Evie had to stop him and ask him to explain. Every time he finger-spelled a word, Evie got confused, and he shook his head at her as he slowly spelled out his words in the air between them again and again.

His mirth was silent, but his eyes sparkled, and his body shook. There was something else in his eyes, too, something that made Evie's stomach clench painfully, made her blush and looked away, only to look up immediately again. Even when she looked away, she could feel his eyes on her, his expression somewhere between surprise and delight. It sent chills through her to think that *she* was the reason he looked so happy.

"Tell me why you learned to sign," Roman demanded, leaning across the desk toward her. Their books were pushed to the side of the table, forgotten. *"Do you have someone deaf in your family?"*

Evie put her hands in her lap, thinking for a minute before she answered. It was the first time he had asked a question about *her*. The first time anyone other than Bea had asked a question about her in a very long time. She had gotten so good at slipping in and out of classrooms. Of looking innocuous and blending in. She planned out her words, checked that everything she was about to say was safe before she let herself lift her hands again. *"It's hard to explain,"* she signed, trying to put into words something she had never articulated before. *"My first semester here, one of the classes I was in had an interpreter. I couldn't stop watching her. It seemed like magic, the way she could write in the air, make the words and ideas turn into movement. I fell in love right away. And I like the quiet. Words sometimes feel so dangerous to me. They can do so much harm. There is something about ASL, though."* She shrugged.

Roman's eyebrows shot up, softly skeptical. *"A person can use sign to be cruel, though,"* he pointed out hesitantly, as though worried that he would offend her. *"I've seen it lots of times. A person can curse in sign, lie in sign . . . do everything in sign that you do with spoken words."*

Evie shrugged. *"I don't know. It's just different."*

"How?"

"I can't explain it." Evie looked away. *"Sign feels different to me. It feels . . . safer."* She blushed.

Roman nodded, then glanced down at his watch. *"It's way past lunch time!"* he signed. *"I can't believe the time's gone by so quickly! Why don't we take a break and get some food?"*

"Oh, no. Um," Evie's fingers fumbled as she tried to think of a

good excuse. *"You go ahead. I'll stay here, and . . ."* Her hands fell, limp, into her lap as he stood.

"Come on." Roman towered over her, shaking his head and beckoning imperiously. *"I owe you for saving my butt and sharing your notes. I'm buying."*

Evie had rules for herself. Rules designed to keep her safe, and unnoticed. Like always knowing three ways out of every building, and never asking questions during class. Rules she knew, deep down, she was breaking now. But it was her birthday, and she was hungry. And when she stood, Roman put his hand on her arm, as though wanting to make sure that she didn't trip as they wove through the study-tables and out of the library's front doors. *Just this once,* Evie promised herself. *Just for today.*

"Okay, fine. You win!" she signed. *"But I'll drive . . . it'll give me a chance to introduce you to my car."*

Walking to her car was a hilarious misadventure. Roman had no backpack to swing over the long, black leather trench coat that he never took off. Evie's bag was already full to bursting, so they had to pass his books back and forth between them, freeing the hands of whoever needed to sign at the moment. Roman was impatient when he wanted a turn, which led him to wave his books urgently in Evie's face and when that failed, he tried to sign with them crammed into his armpits. More than once, they landed in a messy heap on the pavement. Soon they were both laughing so hard that Evie forgot to even look forward to the food.

She felt full already.

They reached the garage, and walked together up the spiraling metal steps, their footsteps loud and echoing strangely. The garage was lonely and silent, dark despite the sunlight that shone just outside, and Evie felt as though she and Roman were the only two people left in the world. The fluorescent bulbs that hung from the ceiling bled the color out of everything, casting strange shadows on Roman's face. They reached the third level and turned to walk to Evie's white, four-door Nissan, waiting in the distance.

"Oh my God."

The books tumbled from her grasp, and her hands flew to her face, clutching at her ears.

"Evie? What's wrong?"

Evie backed away, her eyes bulging as they darted from one shadow to the next, trying to find the danger.

"Run, Roman," she cried, but she didn't sign it. In her terror, she forgot every sign she'd ever known. "Run!"

Roman grabbed her by the shoulders, turning her so she could see his hands, but she wouldn't look at him. Her eyes focused on her car, its doors flung open, glass scattered on the ground.

"What's wrong? What's happened?" he signed urgently.

She shook her head, the panic in her chest building into a scream.

"They've found me. They've FOUND ME!"

MOLLY

There was no time to do anything except try to move out of the way. Molly spun on her heel, turning her body away from the knife. She wasn't fast enough, and the blade sliced deep into her left shoulder, leaving a trail of red behind it, burning as it cut. She screamed, hating the sound even as it ripped out of her gut. It was the sound of weakness. Fear. She disowned it as soon as it passed her lips and covered it with anger.

"What the fuck are you doing?" she screamed. "Stop it, Jake! Wake up!"

Through the anger, she could still hear the shock in her voice, the confusion. Blood coursed down her arm, staining her white tank top, catching in the hair that hung thick around her shoulders. The wound hurt more than she would have imagined, the pain made her eyes water and her head swim.

Jake stood still, panting hard, facing her. For a minute, all Molly could think of was a bull in a ring, the crazed glint of his eyes as he prepared to charge again.

"It's me, Jake!" Molly cried, backing away. Cold dread spread through her. He was like a ghost of himself. It had been weeks since she had seen him, and whatever had happened to him, whatever he had done, the man standing in front of her was little more than a shadow of the man she had known not that long ago. The Jake she had known had been sturdy so she longed to know what it would feel like to have his strong arms wrapped around her. Now he was gaunt, his face hard and sharp around the edges. This man was dirty, where the Jake she had known had always been crisp. When she had known Jake, he had always been careful to keep his head closely shaved; now his head was covered in brittle black fuzz.

Molly had always known that he was a junkie. She didn't need to see the tracks on his arms—she could see the hunger in his eyes. She could see it in the tilt of his head, like he was always searching the room, trying to see a bulge in someone's pocket. But still, she could hardly believe what the drugs had done to him.

"It's me. Molly. You remember me, right? You used to come to my concerts. Every night, you'd stand right by the stage. We used to talk after the show."

He stepped toward her.

"Wait, Jake! What's the matter with you? We're friends. Don't you remember?" She wanted so much to be strong, but she could feel her legs shaking as she backed away from him. Tears were stinging in her eyes.

I'm not crying, she thought. *He doesn't get to make me cry.*

The phrase came to her so easily; a familiar mantra, slipping right back into its old place in her mind, like an old shoe, or a pair of jeans long worn. *He doesn't get to make me cry.* She'd said it so many times. Half defiant declaration, half frightened plea with herself to somehow find strength she wasn't sure she had. A prayer whispered in the dark.

Jake charged, but when he crashed against her, Molly didn't see his face. She saw a man with blond hair slicked back, a smug smile twisting his face into something ugly and cruel. His image swam in front of her eyes as she crashed onto the cement, Jake's body heavy on top of her, her hands tied and useless behind her back. The force of his impact knocked them halfway across the room, so she felt the heat of the fire lick against her face. It was close, too close. She tried to crane her head away, afraid her hair would catch fire, but he held her down with a desperate, wiry strength.

"Stop it," she said, her voice weak. She was dazed, her words slurred. She sounded like a person waking from a dream.

He grunted as he punched her, hard, in the stomach, his fist digging deep into her flesh.

"Stop it!" she cried again, his blow driving air out of her lungs and giving her words more force. He was too heavy and too strong; she was bleeding and bound. She knew she didn't have a chance. The firelight made the knife shine when Jake lifted it high into the air. The blade was already dyed red and slick with her blood. He didn't even look her in the eye as he brought it down on her. It was like she wasn't there, like he wasn't seeing her.

"Stop!"

He heard her, though. The knife pierced the skin just above her breast, and cut deep enough to make her scream.

But it stopped.

This time her scream was one of rage: *"GET OFF ME!"*

She struggled and kicked as he slid to the floor beside her. He still gripped the knife in his hand, kneeling bent over on the ground, frozen and confused. His eyes were bloodshot and clouded.

Molly's arm was throbbing, and she could feel the blood spilling from the gash that ran across it. Her perfect white skin torn—another mark that wouldn't go away. He struck out at her, and she lurched away.

"NO! No one gets to touch me like that. Not anymore."

She felt herself vibrating. But it wasn't with fear. Kick over the smooth white stone of Molly's friendly face, and there was something ugly that burrowed in the dark. Anger, the kind that hurt those who inspired it, that lashed quickly, and with relish.

"Fuck you," Molly muttered, letting out half a sob, closing her eyes as she let the anger out. "Fuck all of you. You don't get to do this to me." She struggled till she managed to get up onto her knees. "I'm not that person anymore. I'm stronger now." Molly stared at Jake, but it wasn't him she saw.

"Look at you," she said with disgust. "It makes you happy to frighten people, doesn't it? You sick *fuck*. I know you. I know what you do. But you can't . . . not to me. I'm too strong. You hear me? You don't get to hurt me anymore. I'm stronger than you."

She struggled to her feet until she stood staring down at Jake. He still knelt, hunched by the flames, staring at the knife in his hand. He looked up at her for a long second, and then in a sudden, clumsy movement, roared and brought the knife around in a savage arc, aiming for her thigh. Molly shouted and kicked furiously, knocking the knife out of his hand. It fell into the fire. Jake let out a wordless howl of rage.

"What, Jake? You want that?"

She kicked him.

"Not done cutting me yet?"

She kicked him again—hard, in the side. He flinched, but didn't look at her; his eyes were fastened longingly on the knife.

"Pick it up then, if you want it so much. Go on, Jake. Pick up the knife. Pick it up. *PICK IT UP!*"

Jake's eyes slid out of focus. He turned with a fluid, sure motion, and thrust his hand into the flame.

There was a second when Molly felt nothing but the thrill of power, the warmth of her strength and safety spreading through her chest, the dizzy joy of knowing what she could do.

Then he screamed.

He screamed a high-pitched cry of unspeakable agony, turning to Molly helplessly with tears streaming down his face. His hand was still in the fire. Molly stood frozen as seconds passed, staring at him and at what she had done.

"Jesus Christ, Jake." She dropped to her knees beside him, at first not understanding. "Jesus, take your hand out of the fire! I didn't mean it! *Take your hand out, Jake!*"

He pulled his hand out, and the knife clattered, smoking, to the floor.

Jake moaned. Where just seconds before there had been a smooth, perfect hand, now there was a blistered, swollen claw, the flesh bright red in some places, and other places charred and black. The burned smell of it filled the room, and Molly felt bile rise in the back of her throat. Jake coughed and sobbed, cradling his ruined hand to his chest.

"Oh my God. I can't believe I did that. Jake, I'm so sorry. SO sorry, Jake. Here, untie me." Molly held her hands out to him. He looked at her, confused.

"I want to help you, Jake. Please."

Jake reached out and, clumsy and one-handed, undid the rope that tied Molly's hands. As soon as she was free, Molly yanked off her tank top and, holding his hand as gently as she could, wrapped her shirt around it like a bandage. Jake shuddered and let her work, leaning into her to keep from falling over. Molly was crying silently, holding his hand in her lap. His skin was warm against hers, as though from a fever. The stubble on his head scraped against the gash on her chest. Molly wrapped her other arm around his shoulder and tried to hold him up.

"I'm so sorry, Jake," she said again, her voice a whisper.

"I'm sorry, too."

Molly jerked with surprise when he finally spoke. His voice was thick and gravelly, but terribly familiar. Her heart twisted. No matter what had happened to him in the weeks they'd been apart, she knew that voice. He was still the person she had known, underneath his fury and fear.

She pulled him tighter against her body, feeling his whole body tremble in her arms.

"I'm sorry, sorry. So sorry," the words choked out as tears streamed down his face. "I didn't know what I was doing. I'm such a mess. I didn't recognize you at first, but I do remember you." He looked up at her, his eyes wide and swimming with tears. "Of course I do. I just . . . I'm hurting so much."

"The burn looks awful."

Jake half laughed.

"Yeah," he said. "But it's the drugs that're killing me. It's so bad I'd do anything to get some." His voice was broken, his words disjointed. "I know I'm fucking dying. I just wish it would happen faster. I wish I could stop making everything worse, hurting the people around me. I just wish that there wasn't so much pain."

He lifted his head and looked at her, his eyes finally clear.

"I do remember you, though. Truth is, I could never forget you."

For a moment, Molly saw Jake as though he was standing in front of the stage, gazing up at her, his eyes glinting as he smiled. She remembered sitting with him after the show, wishing they could be together, wishing he wasn't so messed up and damaged that he practically had a warning label stamped between his eyes. His head was pressed against her shoulder; his skin warm and soft.

Without thinking, she leaned down and kissed him.

Jake turned toward her, pressing against her, hungry for her touch, for her forgiveness, desperate for anything that wasn't pain. She leaned into him, something fierce and harsh passing between them.

Molly's head swam. Inside her a hundred impulses and desires, newly surfaced, fought for control. Fear and adrenaline mixed with the thrill of Jake's body against hers. Without thinking, without knowing how she knew, her lips traveled up his cheek, brushing his skin.

Finding his ear.

"Hear me," she whispered. She kissed him there, before taking his earlobe in her teeth and biting down. Hard. Jake stiffened and

pulled back, crying out softly and struggling, but she bit down harder until she could taste his blood welling in her mouth.

He stopped trying to pull away.

She ran her tongue across his wound, and he moaned, deeply and with pleasure. He convulsed and pressed up against her.

"You're mine," Molly whispered. *"Feel no pain."*

He moaned again. This time the sound was sharper and tinged with shock. She leaned down and kissed his lips again. He fell against her, his head resting on her bare skin. When he looked up, his eyes were wide.

"What did you just do to me?" he whispered, his voice filled with wonder. "I don't feel anything. My hand . . ." He held it up, staring at it, as though he hadn't been sure it was still attached to his body. "It doesn't hurt anymore. And . . . fuck . . . the pain . . . it's gone. What did you do?" He pushed himself closer to her, his eyes urgent. "I can't remember the last time I wasn't hurting. The last time I didn't feel that need. How did you make all the pain go away, just like that?"

Molly stared back at him, her eyes wide, her heart beating a frantic staccato in her chest. "I don't know," she whispered.

At that moment, a door scraped cement, and at the far end of the room, Andrew stood, peering into the semi-darkness.

"Molly?" he called, not seeing. Then his eyes found her. "What happened to you?" He ran toward her, several other people spilling into the room after him.

"You're bleeding!" He stared at her in shock, his eyes traveling from Jake's hand to her shoulder, and finally to the blood-stained knife on the floor.

"He had a KNIFE?"

Molly couldn't doubt the shock on Andrew's face as his eyes ran over her.

"Tyler, what the fuck is going on? The guy had a knife on him!"

Tyler stepped up behind Andrew and looked, his face blank and impassive, at Jake and Molly huddled on the floor.

"You never told me to frisk him, sir," was all he said, and Andrew rolled his eyes in anger, still taking in the scene.

"And . . . oh my God." If Molly had thought Andrew looked surprised before, it was nothing compared to his expression now, as he stared at Jake. Jake stared back at him, blood trickling from his ear, leaving a red streak down his neck.

"You blooded him," Andrew said. It wasn't a question. Molly shook her head, confused.

"I don't know what that means," she said. It was ridiculous, after all that had happened, but she felt embarrassed "I . . . I bit him. I don't know why. He was hurting, and I . . . I just wanted to make the pain stop."

"Holy shit. You blooded him without even being told what to do." Andrew ran a shaking hand through his hair. "He's bound to you now. For the rest of his life. Forever, unless you send him away. You don't even need to use your voice on him. He's bound to obey you all the time. Even if you do send him away, the bond will just fade, slowly. It'll never completely go away." Jake and Molly looked at each other for a long, searching moment. Jake inched closer to her, leaning into her, his eyes pleading. He put his mouth up next to her ear.

"You won't send me away, will you?" he whispered. "Please . . . don't."

Molly turned to him and ran her knuckles over the black fuzz that covered his head. Jake closed his eyes, leaning into her touch.

"Oh, no," Molly answered softly. "I'll keep you."

JAKE

There was light, and the noise of many voices whispering together.

The swish of fabric as legs ran.

Jake sat with his head leaning back against the cement wall behind him. His shoulder pressed against Molly's bare skin; the warmth of her touch was the only thing that felt real. Jake worked hard to keep his eyes open, not trying to understand the swirl of people around him. The thin man, Andrew, the one with red hair that everyone seemed to be taking orders from, stood close by Molly's other side. His voice was the only one that did not whisper. It roared and snapped. First, he had yelled at the dreadlocked man, cursing him, ordering him from the room. Now, he hollered directions at everyone. Everyone obeyed him without a second glance. He seemed ready to fly into a rage. Molly was the only person he spoke to gently, squatting down next to her, touching her bruised face with concern.

Jake felt a wave of self-loathing. All her wounds . . . he had caused them.

"It wasn't supposed to be like this, Molly," Andrew was telling her. "I had no idea he was armed. That he would go after you like that. It was all a terrible mistake. One that could have cost you your life. I am so sorry that it happened. We have someone here—he's a nurse. They're finding him now. He'll be here in just a minute. Just hang on."

Jake knew someone had slipped him that knife, and told him what to do with it. But he didn't say anything. Molly's words had taken away his pain, but they couldn't fix his hand, or stop the shaking that continuously wracked him. He felt like he was floating above his body, as though the black and bloody claw of a hand belonged to someone else. As though the veins that ached with emptiness were not his own.

Somewhere, far away, his body was pulsing with pain. Convulsing with longing. Somewhere close by, a junkie was getting just what he deserved, writhing with anguish that paid him back in full for every moment of ecstasy that drugs had ever bought him. But that person wasn't Jake.

Molly was looking at him, her eyes wide with concern.

"Are you alright?" she asked, and he jerked his head in a nod, reaching out and wrapping dirty fingers around her wrist. The smooth feel of her skin under his fingers soothed him. He would have liked to curl up and put his head on her lap.

"Just keep close," he whispered, his voice hoarse. The crowd parted, and a tall, wiry man with messy brown hair that fell into his eyes hurried forward, setting a medical bag down in front of Molly and leaning over her. He pulled a pair of medical gloves on with practiced ease. When he reached out and touched the gash on Molly's shoulder, she gasped and shied away in pain.

"How bad is it, Matt?" Andrew asked, crouching down to peer at her wound.

Matt sucked in air between his teeth and shook his head. "Pretty bad. Damn near nicked the bone. I'm surprised she hasn't passed out already. Do you feel like you're going to pass out?" he asked Molly, raising his voice a little to get her attention, but keeping it gentle. "If you do, I need you to tell me. I don't want you to fall over and add a concussion to your list of injuries."

"No, I'm alright," Molly answered, her voice faint and her eyes half closed. Andrew watched her closely for a minute, then cursed and straightened himself up, turning away for a moment as the nurse set to work cleaning the wound. When he turned back around, his eyes zeroed in on Jake.

"Thia?" He called, and a blonde woman with a pony tail pulled high at the back of her head darted to his side and looked up at him expectantly. "I think," Andrew said slowly, "it's about time we throw that trash out." He nodded in Jake's direction.

Jake startled and had to fight hard to resist the useless impulse that flared inside him to cling to Molly as hard as he could. He had no right to be here . . . had no right to be with her, especially not after what he had just done. Logically, he knew that. But as panic roiled inside him, he realized he wasn't sure if he was physically capable of walking away. Every instinct in his body was screaming at him to stay by her side.

"No." Molly's eyes flew open. She adjusted herself so that she sat up a little straighter. "Jake stays with me."

"He attacked you," he said sharply. "He tried to take your life. He spilled the blood of an Echo here, in our sanctuary. He can't stay here."

Jake could feel Andrew's anger mounting like the pressure of a storm front bearing down on the people in the room. This man was not used to being argued with, and now he was staring at Molly with fury flashing in his eyes. "It's okay, Molly. Really." Jake hurried to break in before she said anything to make Andrew angry, even though the words hurt to say. He could tell how powerful the man was from the way the others practically cringed away from his gaze. The last thing he wanted was for Molly to put herself in harm's way. "I'll go."

He started to stand up, and Molly turned toward him.

"No," she told him gently. "You're not going anywhere."

And just like that, Jake was sitting back down beside her, the fingers of his uninjured hand intertwined tightly with hers. The sound of her voice made him feel as though he had just taken a shot of aged whiskey. Warmth blossomed in his chest with a feeling of absolute certainty he was exactly where he was meant to be.

"She might be right, Boss," Thia murmured hesitantly. "I thought I'd always heard that folks shouldn't be separated right after they make the blood bond. Couldn't it hurt them, or something?" She made the words a question, but Jake could tell from her expression that she was sure the words were true. "Molly's new here, but she seems pretty powerful. It'd be a shame if something happened to weaken her voice."

Andrew tilted his head to the side, his expression suddenly thoughtful, and Jake realized that Thia had known just the right thing to say.

"Fine," Andrew said, after a moment of consideration. "He can stay. For now."

"You need to look at Jake's hand," Molly said to the nurse, her voice urgent. "He's hurt pretty bad."

Matt had already been casting sidelong glances in Jake's direction as he finished up the last stitches on Molly's shoulder.

"Yeah," he said, "about that . . ." He quickly changed into a fresh pair of gloves and leaned over Jake's hand, gingerly pulling the ash and blood-stained tank top away from his skin. "This is way beyond my skill level," he said. "Seriously. I have a PHD in nursing, and I know when I'm out of my league. An injury like this is light years beyond anything that I can treat on my own. He needs a hospital."

"It's fine," Jake said hurriedly. "It doesn't hurt at all. If you could just bandage it up, I'll be totally fine."

"Okay, *that's* an insane thing to say." Matt rocked back on his heels and looked Jake over appraisingly, as though wondering if he was high right now. "It will not be fine. It needs treatment."

He spread his hands out to either side. "Like . . . a *lot* of treatment."

"Enough," Andrew snapped. "He can stay. For now. Just bandage him up."

Jake saw Matt biting down on his lip to keep from arguing, as he hurried to do as Andrew said.

Thia came over and crouched down next to Molly, a cup of water in her hand. "Here," her eyebrows drew together as she gazed intently at Molly's face. "You should drink something.

"Thank you," Molly said with a tired smile. Then she thrust the cup into Jake's uninjured hand.

Jake shook his head and tried to hand it back. "You need it. You're hurt."

"You're hurt worse than me," Molly pointed out. "You need it more."

"No, really . . ." Jake protested, and Molly rolled her eyes.

"Drink," she ordered.

He drank.

"Geez, calm down!" Thia exclaimed, who had watched the whole exchange and was now looking at them as though they were both insane. "I can get you a second cup of water!"

She got up, muttering to herself, and soon they were both sipping water, while Matt finished wrapping Jake's hand in layer after layer of gauze.

When Andrew's back was turned, Matt leaned forward and whispered in Jake's ear. "If you're still here tomorrow, you come find me, okay? Let me at least take a look at it."

Jake gave a quick nod of agreement.

As soon as Matt finished, Andrew came and helped Molly to her feet. Jake scrambled up after her, trying to stay close. The room felt claustrophobic now that it was filled with so many unfamiliar people. The fire was still burning, making the air stifling and warm, filling it with heavy stench of burning wood.

"Everyone!" Andrew called out, and Jake pressed himself

against the wall, hanging his head down and staring at the floor, wishing he could turn invisible as all eyes turned to the front.

"This is Molly," Andrew announced, his voice echoing in the crowded space. "She is one of us now. I know that you will all welcome her, and help her learn about our life here."

"Welcome!" voices chorused, but Jake saw that Molly did not look up, did not return the tentative smiles the others offered.

Andrew turned to Molly and lowered his voice. "Come on," he said. "Let's get you to someplace where you can rest before you fall over."

Molly gave him a tight-lipped nod, and Andrew turned to lead her from the room. Jake felt panic rise as Molly turned away, felt it push through the empty veins he suddenly remembered were his own. Then she reached back, her hand searching for his. He clung to it, and let her pull him behind her, out into an unfamiliar hallway.

The crowd in the room parted to let them by, and Jake felt the weight of their regard like heat against his skin. He didn't register much after that. He knew Andrew led them down a dim hall and opened the door to a vast room with no windows. Molly stepped inside, and Jake hurried after her, walking over to the wall, pressing against it and sliding down onto the floor. He sighed with shaky relief and pulled his knees up in front of him.

Andrew was looking at him, the revulsion in his eyes not disguised. It didn't surprise Jake or bother him. He saw it all the time.

"Are you sure—" Andrew started to ask, but Molly cut him off.

"We'll be alright," she said. "But we have to rest. Okay?" Andrew nodded, still seeming uncertain, and stepped back. Molly pushed the door shut, leaning against it heavily for a moment before turning, her eyes full of concern, to Jake.

She came and knelt next to him. He was sweating and shaking, his arms clamped around his middle, as though he was afraid his body might fall to pieces at any moment. His teeth chattered against each other. He opened his eyes and smiled weakly when he saw Molly leaning over him.

"Shouldn't you hate me or something?" he rasped. "For trying to kill you, and everything?"

Molly shook her head. "You didn't know what you were doing, and I don't hate you," she said. "I'm worried about you. What's wrong?" She lay a hand against his damp forehead. "Is it your hand?"

Jake closed his eyes. The feel of her hand against his face was incredible. He tried to remember the last time someone had touched him so gently. Nothing came to mind.

"Don't worry about me. I'm okay, really." He shook his head. "I don't feel any pain, like you said. It's just the withdrawal. I've had it before, but I've never gotten to the other side." He half laughed, a bitter, tired sound. Molly nodded, understanding dawning in her eyes. Jake caught her hand in his.

"Listen," he said, bone-deep exhaustion making it hard for him to fight down the raw emotion in his voice. "I don't know what's going to happen after this, but I want you to know, it's been a really, really long time since anyone looked out for me like you did back there with Andrew." He swallowed hard. "It means a lot. Thanks."

Molly's smile was sad as she pressed her hand against his unshaven cheek. She kissed his forehead and then leaned down to whisper in his ear.

"You need to rest now," she said. "Sleep. Sleep sweetly. Sleep until the shaking stops. Until it's over."

Jake looked up at her, a rush of gratitude in his eyes. Then his body hurried to obey her, and sleep pounced on him and swallowed him whole.

MOLLY

Molly startled and woke, sitting up to stare blearily around her. She hadn't been able to do much more than tuck a blanket around Jake's shoulders and throw herself onto the unfamiliar bed before collapsing into sleep. Now she blinked as she tried to take everything in. The bedroom was large, with a high ceiling and walls of faded red and brown bricks. There were no windows, but a lantern on top of the wooden dresser gave off a muted, orange light that left the room pleasantly cool and dim. There were two simple, wooden chairs placed against the wall. The bed was soft beneath her, and at some point while she was sleeping, she had wrapped the light blue comforter all around herself like a cocoon. The only sound she could hear was Jake's steady breathing. Molly rolled over and stared at him. He looked so pale.

She wiggled out of the blankets and slid out of bed, moving as softly as she could so as not to wake him. She crouched down and lay her hand lightly on Jake's forehead. Despite his pallid complexion, he was hot to the touch, as though his body was fighting off a fever. Molly bit her lip and hoped he was alright. If he was going through withdrawal, then sleep was probably the best thing for him. At least he seemed peaceful, his face more relaxed than she had ever seen it.

He'll sleep it off, she told herself. *He'll be fine,* when he didn't stir or respond to her touch. *He just needs some time.*

A hesitant knock tapped against the door, and Molly stood and stared. Her heart rate soared, and for one wild second, her eyes darted around the room, searching for an escape route. Then she shook herself. There was no other way out; she would have to face reality sooner or later. Huddling in the dark would not do anyone any good.

She took a deep breath and opened the door.

"Hi," the woman standing on the other side said with a tentative smile. "I didn't mean to wake you. But I figured you might want to clean up." She held up a small duffel bag.

For the first time since she woke, Molly noticed that her clothes were torn and stained with blood and that her hair stank of smoke.

"Yes," Molly agreed with a frown. "I think a shower would be good. Thanks." She accepted the proffered duffel bag, looking at the woman more intently. Her tight blonde ponytail and dark brown eyes were familiar, but Molly's memories from the previous night were a bit blurry around the edges.

"I met you last night, didn't I?" Molly asked, and the woman's smile broadened.

"Yeah, but I didn't expect you to remember. There was kind of a lot going on."

Molly grimaced. "That's one way to put it, I guess."

"I'm Thia. Come on—I'll show you where the nearest shower is."

Molly closed the door softly behind her and followed the swing of Thia's pony tail down the hall. Twice they passed a place where the hallway opened into another long corridor. Molly glimpsed people hurrying from place to place, and a seemingly endless procession of closed doors.

"How many people are living down here?" she asked, jogging a little to catch up.

"Hmm. Good question." Thia's nose wrinkled as she thought. "I'd say about a hundred and fifty right now, give or take. Here we are. The shower's right through this door. There's soap, shampoo —everything that you'll need is in there. I wasn't sure what size you'd be," she said, pointing at the duffel bag in Molly's hand, "but I did my best. We can get you some things you like better real soon. After you've cleaned up, come see me, and I'll get you some food. The tavern's down the hall and to your right," Thia pointed the way. "You can't miss it, just follow your stomach."

"Thanks," Molly said. "That sounds good—I'm starving."

"See you soon, then." Thia smiled and headed down the hall.

Molly opened the door slowly, half expecting to find the equivalent of the showers from her high school gym class behind it. But the bathroom was meticulously clean and starkly functional, with a full-length mirror hanging on one wall and a pile of clean towels folded neatly on the shelf. Molly sighed with relief as she stepped inside and locked the door behind her. She stripped out of her clothes as quickly as she could, and dived into the water, not bothering to wait till it heated up.

Dried blood had crusted under her fingernails. She had to wash her hair three times before the stink of smoke faded away. She kept finding small cuts and bruises on her body she hadn't even realized were there. The stitches hidden under a thick layer of gauze burned and itched, and it was awkward to try to keep the bandage dry. Still, Molly lingered in the shower until the water had filled the room with steam, letting the hot water course over her skin.

Finally, she stepped out of the shower and stood, dripping, in front of the mirror. She stared at her reflection in the fogged glass and felt as though she was looking at a stranger. Even when she rubbed her hand against the glass, her image was still distorted by the steam and water that clung to the mirror. Molly shivered.

Once already, she had rebuilt her life from the rubble. How many more shockwaves could she take before she fell apart completely?

Abruptly, she turned away from the glass and dried herself off vigorously. She refused to let the absolute craziness of the last twenty-four hours derail her life. Yes, something bizarre had happened to her. Yes, she had some things to figure out. Like how to get the hell out of here, and get herself and Jake away from all this insanity. She couldn't deny that she had done something in the bar, and last night with Jake, that she didn't understand. But she didn't need to understand it to know that she wanted no part of it, or of this world. She had a life waiting for her on the surface —a life she had just about killed herself to build. A life that meant everything to her.

She refused to let it slip away.

These people might say she was one of them, but that didn't mean she had to accept it. She had been just fine before the incident at the bar. She would go back to being just fine again. She was sure she could figure out a way to keep herself from doing . . . whatever she had done.

But she knew she couldn't just scream "I don't want any of this!" and storm out the door. Last night, Tyler had paralyzed her with just the power of his voice. Andrew had forced her to go through the initiation without even breaking a sweat. Brute force wouldn't work. If she tried to force her way out, they'd just stop her. She had to be smart about this. She had to learn enough about this world to figure out how to disengage herself from it.

Locked in that room with Jake, she had felt more helpless than she had in a very, very long time. Now it was time to take back control: of herself, and of what was happening to her. No more letting her voice flow from that deep, dark place inside of herself that made strange things happen. No more letting others force her into a role she didn't want.

She unzipped the duffel bag of clothes that Thia had leant her. Jeans that were just a little too big, several tee shirts with punk rock band names emblazoned on the front, and a well-loved pair of sneakers. Molly pulled them on, grateful that Thia had brought her clothes she wanted to wear. Jeans and a tank top were pretty much her unofficial uniform. The muscles in her stomach unclenched a little now that she was clean and dry, but she thought wistfully of her leather jacket, which she had left backstage at the bar. Not just because her cell phone was tucked into her jacket pocket; she would have loved the familiar feel of it on her shoulders right now—giving her another layer, covering up the bruises and the bandage on her arm. It would have felt like armor.

She pulled her battered wallet from the back pocket of her ruined jeans and then threw her spoiled clothes into the trash can. She spent a minute combing her brown and red-streaked hair out with her fingers. Then she took a deep, steadying breath. In one terrifying night, her life had swerved violently off the rails.

Now it was time to get back on track.

Molly pulled open the door and stepped out into the hall. Steam blossomed out the door and swirled all around her. Wet hair clung to the back of her neck. She squared her shoulders, raised her chin, and strode down the hall into an unfamiliar world.

MOLLY

The rich smell of food and the sizzle of a grill wafted toward her, practically pulling her down the hall. Her stomach sat up and took notice, twisting impatiently as she came to stand before the large wooden doors. Above them hung a sign, hand-painted with flowy, elaborate script that read 'Lost Boys Tavern.' Molly stared at it for a moment before walking in.

"There you are!" Thia called from behind the bar, raising her voice to be heard over the thrum of a metro train thundering by above them. "Come on in. We're open, but no one's up yet." She pointed above her. "That's only the second train of the day. Most folks don't roll out of bed till after the a.m. rush. I've almost got your food ready. You're not a vegetarian, are you? Please tell me you aren't, because I've already started your burger."

"A burger sounds great," Molly replied, navigating around the empty tables and chairs and then slipping onto one of the red leather stools that clustered around the bar. "But isn't it a little early for that?" She was sure it couldn't be later than nine in the morning.

Thia snorted and turned to the grill to give the meat an expert flip. "One of the privileges of living an almost entirely underground existence is getting to eat whatever you want, whenever you want it. Which is why I also suggest a beer." She pulled one from under the counter and popped the top off before setting the frosted bottle down in front of Molly with a bang.

"Oh, now you're speaking my language," Molly groaned, as she grabbed the bottle and gulped half of it down. Thia laughed and slid a plate piled high with spiced fries and a luscious burger across the counter to her.

"This food is amazing," Molly mumbled, her mouth full.

Thia gave a theatrical bow. "We aim to please," she grinned. "With the number of burgers I've made in this place, it would be embarrassing if I hadn't figured out how to get it right by now."

"She's the best burger-maker this side of the Potomac!" a man's voice called out, and then the door from the kitchen clattered open. Molly recognized the gangly man with chin length brown hair spilling into his eyes as the medic who had stitched up her shoulder last night. He was lugging a crate, which he set behind the bar with a huff. "More beer," he grunted as he straightened up and wiped his forehead. "As per your request."

"Thanks, Matt. You're the best." Thia pulled the crate open and stocked the cooler behind the bar.

"Your name's Molly, right?" Matt held out his hand. "Sorry that we didn't get introduced properly last night."

"No worries. Thanks for stitching me up," Molly said, as she shook his hand.

Matt shrugged. "It's what I do. When I'm not helping out behind the bar, that is. Fortunately, my nursing skills are rarely called on around here."

"You two run this place?"

"It's kind of a communal effort, actually," Thia said. "Everybody chips in here and there. Washing dishes, buying supplies. That kind of thing."

"But we're the backbone of the operation!" Matt insisted.

"Without us, the beer would be warm, and the burgers would be overcooked."

"So you have both been down here a while?" Molly asked.

"Yep, for years. And I bet you've got a million questions, don't you?"

Molly nodded.

"I'm not surprised. I've got a few for you myself, if you don't mind. Rumors have been flying about you since last night."

Molly raised an eyebrow. "What kind of rumors?"

Thia leaned a hip against the bar and took out a beer of her own. "They're saying that you didn't know what you are," she said as she pried the cap off her bottle. "They're saying that you threw a loop around a whole room full of people, and then made a blood bond with that guy last night, all while having no clue what you were doing."

Molly took a long sip before answering. She had a feeling that she would need a little alcohol in her system for this conversation.

"They've got it right," she admitted finally.

Matt gave a long, slow whistle.

"You're shitting me!" Thia cried, her hand flying to her mouth. "So you found out about all of this . . . when?"

"Last night."

Matt and Thia stared at Molly, the identical expressions of shock on their faces almost comical.

"Quick, Thia." Matt said in a raspy whisper after a minute. "Get that woman another burger. She needs to build up her strength."

"No, forget the meat," Thia said with a wide-eyed shake of her head. "What she needs is *real* liquor." She reached below the counter and pulled out a bottle of vodka. "I mean, I like it here and all," she gestured around the bar with the bottle still in her hand, "but this shit ain't exactly Diagon Alley."

"Yeah," Molly nodded as she accepted the brimming shot that Thia slid in her direction. "I've been figuring that out pretty fast."

"Okay, so forget the questions I was going to ask you," Thia waved a hand, as though erasing her questions from the air. "What do you want to know? If I know Andrew at all, then I know that you came out of talking with him even more confused than you had been before the conversation started."

"Yeah, that's for sure," Molly rubbed her forehead. "I guess the first thing I'm trying to understand, and this sounds so ridiculous that I can't even believe I'm saying it, is *who* is trying to kill me, exactly? I mean, Andrew kept implying that he had saved my life by bringing me down here, which doesn't even make sense. He kept mentioning 'the Echoes' and 'the Watchers.' I couldn't keep straight who is who, or why any of them would care about me one way or the other."

Thia bit her lip and looked at Matt, giving him a slight, encouraging nod of her head.

"You wanna take a stab at that one?" she asked, and Matt sighed, stepping closer as he raised both his hands as though he was about to begin a great narration.

"Let me explain . . ." he began, his voice taking on a slightly Spanish accent. "No, there is too much. Let me sum up."

"Jesus, Matt!" Thia groaned, slapping herself on the forehead. "This is serious! Now is not the time for Princess Bride quotes."

"Inconceivable!" Matt cried indignantly. "It's always time for Princess Bride quotes!"

Thia lay her head down on the bar and groaned.

"As I was saying," Matt went on, ignoring Thia pointedly, "before being rudely interrupted. Try to think of it this way. This bottle of vodka represents the Watchers." He held up the bottle of vodka before setting it down directly in front of Molly. "They're the full-blooded Sirens."

"So, their powers are super strong, right?" Molly asked. Matt nodded.

"Yup, their power is undiluted. Not anything like what even the strongest of us can do. If one of them speaks to you—even once—even just a word . . . that's the end of the story." He made a slicing gesture over his neck. "You're theirs—forever. No one knows much about them—not even what they look like. They stay in the shadows. They stalk you at night. If they get you, you never come back to tell anyone how it happened. Now this bottle," he held up one of the empty beer bottles and set it side by side with the vodka. "It represents the Legacies. They're the direct result of Watchers and humans getting all freaky with each other a very long time ago."

"Matt!" Thia moaned. "Why can't you be serious about this?"

"I am serious," Matt insisted with a sniff. "Don't interrupt me when I'm disseminating knowledge. So, a long time ago a bunch of Watchers did the nasty with a bunch of humans, and they had little Siren-human hybrid babies. Those babies grew up to realize that, though the power of their voice didn't last long, they could still force humans to do what they wanted with their words, which seemed pretty awesome to them. So, they hung out with each other and formed houses. Legacies married other Legacies. They had their own little Legacy babies. Over the generations, they amassed a ton of wealth and power, forming small dynasties and becoming real assholes in the process. But they do have a problem. Over time, the genetic oomph that the Sirens had given them began to run out. And they kept marrying each other in an attempt to 'keep their blood pure.' Which is always, like, a *super* stellar idea. And at the end of all their inbreeding and feeling superior bullshit, they ended up with a ton of money and a ton of people, and a low level of wide-spread insanity kind swimming around happily in their screwed up, inbred, genetic cocktail. Also, they've got a much smaller degree of actual supernatural power. Despite everything they've done, over time their powers have weakened."

"Except for Steele," Thia cut in, and Matt waved at her to be quiet, wrinkling his nose.

"There's an exception to every rule. There's no need to scare this poor woman silly, and stop interrupting me."

"Fine." Thia took a sulky sip of her beer.

"Now let me see," Matt narrowed his eyes as he looked around the bar. "Ah. Perfect. Do you see that fly?" He pointed at a fly that crouched on the counter top, rubbing its little hands together.

"Yes?" Molly answered, not sure where Matt was going with this.

"The fly is us." Matt said, and, in a lightning fast movement, he picked up the beer bottle and slammed it down. The fly darted into the air, narrowly avoiding being splattered on the counter top. "Oh, it's nice that he got away." Matt said thoughtfully. "It makes the demonstration a bit less gruesome than I had expected. Anyway, the point is, and to answer your original question: *we* are the Echoes. And *everybody* wants to kill us. The Legacies want to kill us because we aren't part of any of their houses. They think of us as scum because we're not part of their blood lines, and as a security risk because they're afraid that we'll expose them to the world and they'll lose the power that they've spent generations accumulating. I mean, it isn't a coincidence or anything that three of the largest Legacy households are based right here in DC. If there's a pie that they don't have their fingers in, it's because there isn't enough power or money *in* that pie for it to be worth their time."

Molly swallowed, still staring at the spot on the counter where the fly had been just a moment ago. "Okay. But what about the Sirens?"

"We prefer to call them Watchers." Matt said with a little shrug. "It's just so much more modern that way."

"Oooookay. Fine. So, what about the Watchers? Are they after you, too?"

"You mean 'us'." Thia chimed in helpfully. "And yeah, for sure the Watchers are after us. They try to keep a lid on the Legacies, giving them rules and all kinds of restrictions on what they can or cannot do. But we're not part of the Legacies houses. So, we're breaking their rules just by existing."

"And you can't join the Legacies houses, because they want to kill you?"

"Want to kill *us*," Thia smiled like Molly was an elementary school student doing well on a math quiz. "That's right."

Molly rubbed her eyes roughly. "Alright, so there's a lot here that I don't understand, and even more that I don't even want to think about, but there's one thing that just really doesn't make sense. If Echoes aren't Watchers or Legacies, then where does their power come from?"

"Genetics can be a real bitch," Matt said with a shrug. "People are running around out there right now." He pointed above his head, toward the metro system and surface. "They're happy in their ignorance. They don't realize that they've got the genes for these powers, buried deep inside their DNA. And then, for some of them, those genes wake up. They start to express themselves. And then, before you know it, you're using your voice to get all you ever wanted one minute, and then running like hell for your life the next."

"The genes just wake up?" Molly asked, her eyebrows climbing. "How? Why would that happen?"

"Trauma." Thia explained, her voice matter-of-fact. "Really bad, God-awful trauma. Those abilities are buried deep, but if you're in bad enough trouble, your body starts to dig them out. Like a defense mechanism. Or like a pot of soup—the fat rises to the top when soup starts to boil. All of us Echoes started as regular people. And then shit happened, and slowly, things began to change. Which means that not only do we have our fabulous, powerful voices in common, but we're also all really screwed up in the head!" She smiled brightly.

"The good part," Matt said, leaning his elbows against the counter, "is that we've missed out on all the inbreeding and the slow, generational decline that the Legacies have experienced.

That means that our voices are often actually stronger than theirs."

"The bad part is everybody wanting to kill us. And the trauma part." Thia frowned. "Everybody down here has been through hell in one way or another. Hence the name," she gestured toward the 'Lost Boys Tavern' sign.

"I was in an accident," Matt piped up. "I was driving to my job at NIH and got hit by a semi whose driver fell asleep at the wheel. I don't remember much of anything, but they told me that my car flipped over three times, before crashing and catching on fire. I woke up in the hospital with five broken bones, burns over thirty percent of my body, and some burgeoning supernatural abilities." He smiled, but the expression looked forced. Molly stared at him, her mouth hanging open a little. She couldn't even think of how to respond.

"My boyfriend got murdered right in front of me," Thia said, the casual tone of her voice not matching at all the sudden glistening in her eyes. "Gangbangers shot him right in the head. I was in a real dark place for a long time after that—there are whole days, even weeks, that I honestly can't remember at all. Grief sucked me under the surface for a long time. When I got my head back above water, things were different." She touched her chest. "*I* was different."

Silence fell between them, and Molly felt dread building as both Thia and Matt turned to her.

"What about you?" Thia asked her with a gentle smile.

Molly's heart rate sped up. "Nothing," she said, hearing how false her voice sounded. "I can't think of anything like that."

"You don't have to be shy," Thai urged. "Everybody down here has got a story to tell."

Molly didn't remember deciding to stand up, but her stool scraped noisily against the floor as she pushed away from the counter and sprang to her feet.

"Thanks a lot for the burger," she said hurriedly. She pushed the empty plate back toward Thia, ignoring the surprised expression on her and Matt's faces. "It really was good. And thanks for talking to me about things—it was really helpful. I've got to go find Andrew," she lied. "He said he wanted to see me."

Before they could respond, Molly spun on her heel and rushed out the tavern door. Blood was pounding in her ears, and she could feel sweat trickling down the small of her back. She couldn't have explained why her heart was racing, but she knew that she had to get away.

She ran down the hall, ignoring the stares of the few people she passed. When she got back to the bedroom, she flung the door open and darted inside. Jake was still sleeping, sitting on the floor, slumped against the wall with a blanket tucked around him. Molly dragged one of the wooden chairs next to the dresser and wedged it beneath the door knob. Then she sat down heavily on the floor next to Jake.

I'm fine, she told herself fiercely. *I'm healed. Thia and Matt are just wrong. Nothing that happened changed me. I'm still the same person I've always been.*

She leaned back against the wall and closed her eyes, wrapping her arms around herself. She felt tears coming, and she hated them, and herself for being weak. The past was the past. She would not let it touch her, or change her. She had wiped it away, as though those years had never been.

Still, a feeling like grief rose inside her, and her shoulders shook as tears she did not want to acknowledge streamed down her checks.

When she opened her eyes, Jake was looking at her.

"It's okay," he whispered. He moved closer and Molly leaned against him, letting out a breath she hadn't realized she was holding. "You aren't alone," Jake said softly. "I'm here with you. You'll be alright."

He lay his hand on top of hers, and their fingers intertwined.

Molly held on tight, and Jake nestled his head against her shoulder.

"I'm sorry," he said. "I think I need to sleep some more."

"It's fine," Molly smiled, and immediately his eyes closed. "Sleep as long as you need to," she whispered. She looked over at the door. "And as soon as you're done resting, you and I are going to get the hell out of here."

EVIE

"*Go, Roman!*" Evie forced her fingers to move, though her signs were blurred by the shaking of her hands. "*Get out, fast. Run!*"

"*There's no one here,*" he signed back to her, an incredulous smile turning up the corners of his lips.

"*You don't understand,*" Evie pushed against his chest, trying to force him to move back toward the staircase, but she couldn't move him. "*You don't know what they'll do. I'm telling you, they're here. They've come for me.*"

"*Look, Evie.*" Roman grabbed her by the shoulders and spun her around. "*There's no one here,*" he signed. He stepped past her, and gestured broadly around them. "*Absolutely no one.*"

Evie stilled. She held her breath as she pivoted slowly on her heel, her heart racing as her eyes probed every shadow and corner. She saw the scattered, broken glass, gleaming glumly in the garage's weak, neon light. The door of her car had been left hanging open. Someone had riffled through her things.

Could it really have just been a break-in?

"*You're right,*" she signed after a minute. "*It couldn't be them. They never would have left. They'd be here waiting."* Evie pressed her hands to her eyes and fought down a sudden urge to laugh.

Roman tapped her on the shoulder, his eyes narrow. Even though he couldn't hear her talking to herself, she knew she must look crazy.

"Did they take much?" he asked, and Evie couldn't control the hysterical giggle that slipped from her lips.

"I'm sure whoever did this was very disappointed," she signed, not sure if she was crying or laughing. *"There was nothing here to take."*

"Do you want to call the police?"

Evie shook her head vehemently. *"I can't talk to the police."*

"Okay," he said, raising his hands to show he wouldn't pressure her.

"I'm sorry for freaking out," she signed, though she flubbed the movement a little; she felt clumsy and thick-fingered. Roman seemed to understand her anyway. *"It isn't as bad as I thought it was. Like you said, just a break-in."* She ran her hands along the roof of the car, caressing it. "Poor Luna," she murmured. This car was her refuge, her escape route. She thought of it almost as a friend.

"Well, if you don't want to call the police, let's go and get something to eat. You need some food, and you don't want to drive this—not with the glass everywhere. I'll call my driver and have him pick us up."

"Your driver?" Evie asked, and Roman shrugged, the unapologetic motion of a person who took his wealth entirely for granted.

He slid his phone out of his pocket, and his fingers flashed over the keys as he sent a text.

Evie had suspected that Roman was wealthy. Partly from the way he dressed, partly because he seemed so very confident. But still, when the limo pulled into the parking garage and came to a stop in front of them, Evie was left nearly speechless.

*"Is this **yours**?"* she asked, her eyebrows climbing.

This time, Roman had the decency to look a little embarrassed. He nodded. *"We have to use a driver—my brother and I don't have American driver's licenses."*

"Of course," Evie signed, shocked to find herself laughing again as she slid into the cars soft, cocoon-like leather interior. *"And riding the metro or the bus just wouldn't be an option."*

Roman smirked and slid in after her. Evie snuggled into the seat warmers as the limo pulled out of the garage and into traffic. Downtown DC slid by, damp and dirty in the late November wind, but inside the limo, Evie felt a sense of safety and relief spreading through her. The driver lowered the window between the front and the back, just long enough to hand them each a steaming Styrofoam cup, and the smell of espresso and expensive leather filled the air.

She was disappointed when they pulled up in front of the restaurant a few minutes later. She had been enjoying the ride and was sorry it was over—until she realized Roman had taken her to Sandy's.

Sandy's was a favorite hangout for the college crowd, and she had heard it mentioned often in conversations among the other students. Quiet enough for studying, but hip enough for those with no particular interest in academics, it lured a steady stream of students off campus and into the city with its promise of cold beer and late hours. Evie had walked by it once. The smell of pizza that radiated out of it was so seductive that she had felt a positive surge of pride that she did not let her eyes wander longingly to the door. It had old-fashioned, swinging wood doors, like an old-style saloon, and windows tinted like a cathedral.

Roman installed her in a corner booth, far in the back. The polished wood stretched up behind her; the smell of gourmet pizza was thick and soothing, like incense in a temple. Roman went to the front to order their food. Evie could see him, typing out words on his hand-held and holding it up to the waiter, who was nodding and writing things down.

Her phone buzzed in her pocket. Evie pulled it out.

"Can you pick me up at 9:00?" Bea's text asked, and Evie shook

her head, ashamed at herself. She had almost forgotten her promise to her friend.

"Of course," she answered, then hesitated. *"Unless you mind broken windows? My car got broken into, but I can clean it out and at least tape up the windows before I pick you up."*

"Are you alright?!!?" Bea responded immediately.

"Fine," Evie reassured her. Her fingers hovered uncertainly for a moment before she continued. *"Actually, I'm having dinner with Roman."*

"Ugh! Watch out for that creep." Bea warned. *"After the way he's been ogling you all semester . . ."*

"He has not been ogling me!"

"Staring at obsessively might be a better description. I think I actually saw him drooling once. Make sure he doesn't slip anything in your drink."

"He isn't like that!" Evie typed rapidly, frowning. *"He's actually super nice and sweet and . . . handsome."*

There was a brief pause before Bea's response appeared on the screen. *"Hold on . . ."* she wrote. *"I'm trying to find the 'puking' emoji . . ."*

"Oh, hush!" Evie laughed in spite of herself. *"I'll see you in the morning."*

"'Kay," Bea sent back, and Evie slipped her phone back into her pocket.

Roman sat across from her, followed closely by a waiter carrying two beers, who asked to see Evie's ID before setting hers down on the table. Evie blushed and fumbled as she pulled open the front pocket of her book bag and went fishing for her wallet. The ID was fake, but today really was her birthday, and she hoped the waiter wouldn't be suspicious. He gave it a cursory glance, and Roman took it back from him, his eyes running over it as he handed it back to Evie.

Roman pushed the beer across the table to her. *"It'll help you calm down,"* he signed, and held his bottle out, waiting to clink against hers. Evie hesitated, and then picked up her drink and brought it up to tap against Roman's. She winced at the bitter taste but was thirsty enough to keep sipping.

Roman leaned across the table toward her, his face urgent.

"Back in the garage, you kept saying, 'They've found me. They've found me'," he signed. *"Who's the 'they'?"*

"That's funny," Evie signed, smiling. *"I didn't know you could read lips!"*

Roman's whole body stiffened, his nostrils flared, and his eyes flashed with shock.

Evie didn't notice. Her stomach was empty except for the beer she was drinking, and her head felt fuzzy. The waiter brought their pizza to the table, and she thought she might cry at the sight. Thick, hand-made crust and bubbling gourmet cheese. She pulled a slice toward herself and closed her eyes as she chewed the first bite. Her whole body warmed.

"You didn't answer my question," Roman pointed out a minute later.

"Sorry. What did you ask me?"

"Who's the 'they' that you're so afraid of?"

"Oh." Evie grimaced and wished she was a better liar.

"Nobody. I just grew up in a small town, so I'm always afraid of crime here in the city."

Roman hesitated, his brows knitting together as he thought. *"I'm worried about you."* He admitted finally. He reached out to touch her arm, but then pulled his hand away. *"You seemed so afraid."*

Evie shook her head but smiled. He was so kind to be concerned about her.

"Don't you have anyone who can help you?" Roman asked persistently, apparently still not reassured. *"What about your parents?"*

Evie chewed her pizza, trying to think of how to answer. No

one at school had ever questioned her about her life. She made sure that no one paid her much attention. Now Evie wished she had been more careful, had spent time coming up with a cover story convincing enough to tell Roman as he leaned toward her, his eyes burning with curiosity. But her whole body felt weak and disjointed, partly from the ebbing rush of adrenaline, and partly from the now empty beer she still held in her hand.

She couldn't think of anything to tell him but the truth.

"Listen, Roman. My parents are alive and, I hope, well. I just want to keep as much distance as possible between them and me, and if they could be under the impression that I had died in a plane crash, or thrown myself under a train or something like that, it would probably be for the best. Barring that," Evie waved her hand vaguely in the air, searching for the right words, *"I keep a low profile."*

"Low profile," Roman repeated, his brows knit together as he tried to understand. *"What does that mean?"*

Evie threw her hands up in the air, a wordless, helpless gesture.

"It means no credit cards. No bank account. I don't use my social security number; I won't sign a lease or have an e-mail account. The only work I can get is a shift now and then at the coffee shop on 2nd street—Mr. Jensen is the only one who'll pay me in cash."

Roman looked at Evie for a long moment. He looked down at the pizza in front of them. Evie had eaten more than half of it already. She saw understanding flash in his eyes.

"You're hungry," he signed. It wasn't a question.

Evie looked at him, refusing to blink. *"Yes,"* She kept her face emotionless. She would not feel ashamed. Lots of good people were poor. She hadn't done anything wrong.

Roman stared back at her for a minute. *"I'll be right back,"* he signed.

When he returned a minute later, he had a basket of chicken wings in his hand and a second beer tucked under his arm. He slid it over to her and set the chicken in front of her as well.

"I don't need charity," Evie said, feeling blood rise in her cheeks.

"It isn't charity if it comes from a friend," Roman replied, leaning over and brushing his fingers against her cheek. *"I want you to think of me as a friend, Evie."* And then he put something else on the table, a small second plate that he had been hiding behind his back.

It was cake.

A huge piece of chocolate cake, thick with frosting.

"Happy Birthday, Evie." Roman smiled as he sat back down. *"I saw the date on your ID before."*

It was ridiculous that she was crying.

Evie was horrified by the traitor tears rushing down her cheeks, at the sob that, from nowhere, had suddenly materialized in her chest and was pushing steadily up, into her throat, threatening to break out and into the air and expose her. She grabbed for a napkin and turned away in the seat, trying to hide in the corner of the booth. She picked up a fresh napkin and rubbed her face, hard, till her cheeks were bright red and perfectly dry.

"I'm sorry," Roman's hand was on the table, stretching out to her. *"I didn't mean to make you cry."*

She touched his fingers lightly. *"Don't be sorry,"* she signed. *"That's the nicest thing anyone has done for me in a really, really long time."* She reached for a chicken wing and took a slow, rapturous bite. *"And these are delicious."*

Roman pushed her drink closer to her, and obediently she took a long drink.

"So . . . what? You're in hiding or something?" Roman guessed, with insight that took Evie by surprise. She choked a bit on her drink and mopped her chin with a napkin.

"I'm sorry Roman, but I can't . . ." her fingers stuttered. *"I mean, I don't want to . . ."*

"That's okay. I'm sorry. I didn't mean to pry." Roman sat back in his seat. *"It's your business. You don't have to tell me."* But there was

no resignation on his face. His teeth were set tightly together, an expression of grim determination in his eyes.

"Thank you for understanding." Evie signed. *"And for the food."*

"Don't thank me," Roman responded, the terse words flying from his fingers. Then he stopped himself. Evie could practically see him force himself to relax. Under his leather trench coat, his shoulders loosened, and his eyes lightened. *"Did I already tell you about what happened when I accidentally registered for a musical appreciation course?"*

Evie laughed as she shook her head, and for a while time stopped while they ate and laughed together.

She was just scraping the last bits of frosting off her plate when a waiter banged chairs against the table tops, looking their way significantly as he cleaned up for the night. They were the only customers still left in the restaurant. Evie looked down at her watch. *"Wow, I had no idea. We should really go. It's 1:00 a.m. They're going to start throwing things at us if we don't leave soon."*

Roman chuckled and nodded as he slid from the booth, holding the door to the outside open for Evie to walk through. The limo was waiting right were they had left it. Roman opened the door and stood, waiting for Evie to climb in.

"That's okay," The night had grown colder, and the chill startled Evie. She felt more awake than she had a moment ago. She wished that she had worn her coat. *"I've got my metro card with me. There's a metro station just one block down. I'll be fine."*

"I can give you a ride back to your car," Roman protested, and he straightened as something else occurred to him. He took a step back, toward her. *"Where are you sleeping tonight, Evie?"*

Evie wasn't sure what he was asking. *"I'll be okay. You don't have to worry about me. I've got to go—I'm taking my friend to a doctor's appointment in the morning."*

Roman leaned closer so she could feel the warmth of his body wafting up against her.

"Where are you sleeping tonight, Evie?" he asked again. Now there

was no question in her mind what he was asking. What he offered.

She smiled, stepping away as she shook her head. *"See you in class, Roman,"* she signed, then turned her back on him, pulling her thin jacket tighter around herself as she hurried down the street.

BEA

The run was a joke—Bea knew that before she made it to the end of the block. Still, she forced herself to keep going, made one leg move and then the other, all the while cursing herself under her breath. She had known it even before she left. When it had hurt so much and taken so long to tie her fucking shoelaces. But she wanted this. Wanted it back. She had missed the pavement and the movement, the freedom that had been such a part of her life. Before. She had wanted so badly to feel the wind on her face one more time.

She made it less than a quarter of a mile. She knew exactly how far she had gotten, years of triathlons and long, countryside runs had taught her how to measure distances.

"Fuck it," she said at last, and she let herself stop. She stood for a minute with her hands on her hips, breathing hard, feeling the unnatural looseness of her running clothes around her body. Everything hurt. She couldn't do it.

Her feet dragged as she turned back, her pace picking up a little when she saw Evie's car parked in front of her house.

"You weren't kidding about the broken windows," she commented. Evie was standing beside the car, duct tape in hand, trying to make sure that the plastic she had stretched over the now empty window panes stayed in place.

"I know. Lovely, isn't it?" Evie turned to her with a rueful smile.

"So, how did things go last night between you and our trench coat-clad friend?"

"Fine," Evie answered, rolling her eyes a little.

Bea arched her eyebrows as she gestured for more information. "That's the vaguest answer ever," she pointed out. "You've got to give me a little more than that."

"It was nice," Evie looked down at her shoes. "He bought me cake."

"Chocolate cake?"

"Yep."

Bea sniffed. "Well, that isn't too bad, I guess. Maybe he isn't a complete loss." She rubbed her arms, feeling the late morning chill biting at her skin. "I'm going to go inside and change real quick. Then we can get going."

"Should I just wait out here?"

"I would if I were you. If you come inside you'll have to deal with my parents, and it's like night of the living dead in there. Just long empty silences and dead-eyed stares."

"Okay, yeah," Evie grimaced. "I'll be fine right here."

"See you in a few."

Bea left Evie outside and slammed through the front door with her eyes fixed on the floor. She didn't want to look up and risk meeting her mother's constantly tear-filled eyes, or all her old trophies lined up on the shelves. She clattered into her bedroom, shut the door and locked it. Then she went to the bathroom, pulled off her shirt, and stood staring at herself in the mirror.

She still couldn't quite believe it.

There shouldn't have been a lump. Holy fuck, people her age weren't supposed to get breast cancer. She was twenty-three years old, for Christ's sake! When you're twenty-three, you worry about date rape and drunk drivers. You get wrapped around a car fender while riding your bike. You catch an STD. Breast cancer happened to middle-aged administrative assistants and stay-at-home moms.

This logic had failed to impress her doctors.

When she had first found out, she had been incredulous, more than anything else. She couldn't quite believe that the doctors were right. Her breasts had always been her ally. A tool she wielded skillfully in low-cut dresses and tight tank tops. A weapon she used to get her way, or to get guys she wanted into bed. Suddenly, without warning, her own body had turned against her, swung the shotgun back around and planted it firmly against her temple, poised to blow her brains out all over the street.

But there wasn't just one lump. The cancer was on both sides.

Bea ran her fingers across her chest, against the wounds that had not quite healed. It had been her decision. She had told them to cut them both off. What was the fucking point, anyway? She wasn't going to pretend that she didn't want to live. She wanted it. Wanted it bad. Not that she had a ton of spot-on specific plans, but she was pretty sure there was lots of stuff she hadn't gotten around to doing yet. She'd just as soon stick around, thanks. And she didn't think she'd care, at least not very much. But after the surgery, when she woke up and her hands went *there* and found nothing, she sobbed and threw up anyway. It wasn't the physical pain. That sucked too, but that wasn't it. Her body had betrayed her. Was leaving her. Leaving her with nothing, stripping itself away from her layer by layer with lightning speed before she was finished using it.

The surreal feeling didn't last too long. It had been a shield that her brain instinctively threw up between her and reality—disbelief, denial, whatever—but it wasn't strong enough to hold. The constant haze of pain that came with the chemo and the constant, churning sickness that seemed to have taken permanent residence in her gut, had burned the disbelief away.

At first, there had been reasons to be hopeful. Bea was young and fit. It seemed like they had caught things in time. But then, not long after the surgery, they found the cancer in her lungs. They rushed to start the chemo, even before she was done healing from the surgery. They couldn't afford to wait. And then, slowly, the way the doctors were talking changed.

No one talked about remission anymore. They talked about quality of life. They talked buying time. But no one would just come right out and say it.

Bea felt as though there were two parts of her brain: the part that still didn't quite think it was true, that still wanted another round of chemo, that still thought about going back to work and falling in love and all the white picket fence crap she hadn't even wanted when she was healthy. Then there was the other half. The half that had always, somehow, even before she ever got sick, known this was coming. This part of her wasn't hopeful, wasn't scared . . . wasn't even sad. This part of her was just *pissed.*

She opened the medicine cabinet. There were so many pills. One by one, she choked them down, giving herself an extra dose of the pain-killers, just for a little extra help. Occasionally, she also helped herself to a shot or two of the vodka she kept hidden under her bed. It wasn't exactly doctor-recommended to mix liquor with all the other stuff she was on, but she felt like shit all the time anyway, and at least with the liquor her misery felt a little softer around the edges. She couldn't have anything to drink now, though.

Today she had decisions to make.

Panic swelled in her tender chest. She needed a pause button, a freeze mode, some time when she could step away from the pain and the misery and fucking think. But cancer doesn't give time-outs.

She looked at herself in the mirror. She still recognized herself, even without the prosthetics. She refused to wear them, and she refused to call them that. She called it like it was, and those things were plastic boobs. She wasn't buying. But her eyes were the same deep chestnut shade that had always stared back at her from the mirror. There was just a tiredness there now. And fear.

She remembered what it had been like, the day before she started chemo. She had stood in this exact spot, gazing at her reflection for a good long time. Drinking it in. She had committed herself to memory. The way her hair framed her face, the redness of her checks. Everything. She was so God-damned beautiful that she had to wipe the tears away with the back of her hand. Then she had carefully pulled her hair into a long ponytail, and chopped it off. Then she took her dad's beard trimmer, set it to the lowest setting, and shaved the rest off. She would not go halfway with this thing. She knew where this was headed, and she would damn well look it in the eye. She shoved her ponytail into an envelope and wrote WIGS 4 KIDS on the label. Let the kids have it. She could fucking do without.

Bea could feel how much her body had changed since that day as she pulled on jeans and a tee shirt. She wasn't quite sure what she ought to wear. What was considered appropriate attire for an in-depth conversation about the pros and cons of having noxious chemicals pumped into your body, hoping it would kill something growing inside you before it killed you, too? She wasn't sure.

The whole time she was dressing she knew her parents were in the living room. Just sitting. She could feel them, their anxiety, their grief. It was pressing on the walls and seeping underneath her bedroom door.

Bea couldn't stand it.

She had moved back home after the surgery, and spent hours lying on the twin bed in her old room, reading the Dragonlance books she had been obsessed with when she was a teenager. Her parents loved her, but could hardly look at her now without crying. Bea wanted to yell at them, to throw her thick paperback books at their faces and scream, "I'm the one that's fucking dying! Can you please keep your own shit together, just for me?" But she didn't say that; of course she didn't. Instead, she sat with them through long, painful silences, in front of the TV no one was watching. She had been close with her parents. They loved each other. Probably, if life had been different, she would have gotten married or pregnant, and they would have stopped over at her place and taken the kids out to the park. Happy shit like that. But the sickness pushed it, tested their closeness, picked at it in a way it couldn't withstand.

It was a question their love couldn't answer.

She braced herself before stepping out of her room and, just as she had known they would, her parents turned their incessantly-watery eyes to her, their misery shining like two pairs of million-watt bulbs, pinning her where she stood.

"Where are you going?" her mother asked. "Is that your friend outside? What's her name again?"

"Evie," Bea reminded her. "Yeah, that's her. She and I are just going out for a bit."

They would have freaked out if they knew that she was going to the doctor without them. Her conscience needled her, but she was over eighteen—she had every right to go by herself if she wanted to. The doctor would keep their conversation between just the two of them.

"Are you sure that's a good idea?" her dad leaned forward, his tone immediately anxious. "You're supposed to start your next round of . . . treatment . . . in a week. Don't you think you should rest and save your strength?"

Why did they act like 'chemo' was a bad word? Like, if they didn't say it out loud, it would somehow be less real? Bea shook her head and tried to force a smile. "Don't worry. I'll be fine. I've got my cell phone with me. I'll call you in a bit."

She strode past them, letting the door slam shut behind her as she hurried down the front steps. She threw herself into Evie's car, closing the door more forcefully than she had meant to. A single shard of glass tumbled down from the remnants of the shattered window and fell on the floor by her feet.

"You okay?" Evie asked quietly.

Bea leaned her head back against the seat and closed her eyes as she shook her head.

"Absolutely not," she answered. "Let's go."

Evie pulled out into the street immediately, and drove for a minute before asking, "Where are we going, exactly?"

"To the clinic. Here," Bea tugged her cell phone out of her pocket, and turned on her GPS. "Just follow these directions."

"Sure."

"I don't have chemo today, or anything. I just need to talk to the doctor. I have some questions that I need to ask. Like how much time we're actually talking about here. Like how bad it really is, no holds barred, no more bullshit, just level with me and say it straight out for Christ's sake."

She could feel Evie looking over at her, but Bea closed her eyes again and refused to meet her gaze. After a minute, Evie asked, "Do you want me to come in with you when you talk to the doctor? I probably won't understand most of the medical stuff . . . but I could at least keep you company."

"No," the word sound harsher than Bea had intended it to. "Thanks, though. But I need to do this on my own."

The drive didn't take long, and soon they were parking in front of the building.

"Do you mind just waiting here?" Bea asked, when Evie climbed out of the car. "I don't mean to be rude, I just . . ."

"Bea." Evie cut off her apology, and reached over and caught her hand. "This is about you. Whatever you need, whatever makes this even a tiny bit easier . . . that's what I want to do."

Bea wasn't sure why Evie's words made her throat feel tight, but she nodded her thanks before turning and dashing into the building by herself.

The doctor didn't keep her waiting for long. And when Bea

asked for the truth, he looked her in the eye, steady, and told her just how bad it was. It took her breath away, just knowing. Knowing, without all the medical jargon, all the "maybes" and "we think" and the thousand and one disclaimers that usually cushioned and hid whatever actual information the doctors told her.

She was dying. Probably, it would happen soon.

It shocked her to realize how helpless the doctors were, how many things they couldn't predict, couldn't even really guess about. The chemo could give her more time. There was no way to know how much. And no matter what, it would by crappy time, sick time, time spent shuttling between the clinic and the hospital and the bed in her parents' house. Bea felt an icy feeling slide over her as the doctor spoke. It was a time she didn't want.

The surgery, the chemo . . . all of it had been too late. Life had been a sweet, heady drink, but she was at the dregs already. All that pain and the treatment still hadn't gotten any purchase. End of the road, folks. Thanks for riding. Don't forget your bags. She shook his hand and thanked him for respecting her enough to tell her the truth.

"I won't be back, of course," she added, and to her surprise, he didn't argue or try to change her mind. He patted her on the shoulder with something like compassion, or a close carbon copy thereof, and wished her luck.

She walked out of his office in a daze, wondering how many patients of his were dying, how many conversations like this one he'd had that day. What kind of pills did the good doctor have stocked in his medicine cabinet? Or maybe it stops feeling depressing after a while. Maybe he had already forgotten all about her and was thinking about the Netflix show he was going to binge-watch after dinner. She stepped out onto the sidewalk, and Evie was there, her hands clasped together in front of her, her expression saying plainly that she already knew that the news wouldn't be good.

"How bad is it?" Evie whispered.

Bea just shook her head. "I'm sorry. I can't . . . I can't do this . . ." she stammered, and then she turned and walked away as quickly as she could, leaving Evie behind without a backwards glance. People were streaming out of downtown office buildings, moving in large amorphous clusters toward the metro station, and Bea let them twist around her and carry her along. She stepped on the escalator and the metro swallowed her up, its neck stretching up to envelop her and pull her into oblivion.

She boarded the first train that pulled into the station and rode for a long time. She didn't know where she was exactly, but that didn't matter. She just needed to think. And she watched the people.

There were so many, stepping on and off, checking their phones and jostling for the best seats. All of them had that precious thing she didn't anymore: a future. Life.

I always assumed that I would live, she kept thinking to herself. *I thought I would.*

It had seemed so obvious, so basic. Now the world tottered and prepared to tip over on its side, just as she was catching on for the first time. She gazed out the metro window. The sky peeked at her from between the buildings, a clear, piercing blue, cleaner and purer than she could remember it ever being before. It made her heart ache to see it. Even the passengers around her were beautiful. The elderly black lady, softly balding, who sat reading her paper with a precise, prim dignity. The hilarity of the woman who had missed her calling, and instead of being the prostitute fate clearly intended her to be, wore her business casual clothing so tightly that her body seemed ready to carry picket signs in protest, her face painted so heavily that Bea wondered if she was coming home from the office or heading off to war. A pair of insanely unattractive people, very much in love, laughing and holding hands and seeing in each other beauty that no one else in the whole wide world could see.

It seemed hard to be losing this. To have to say goodbye to the variety, the insanity, the comedy. To life. But there was no more denying what would happen. Bea said it to herself firmly, many times, to be sure she squelched any last resistance.

"I am going to die."

She whispered it over and over, half hoping that the person sitting in front of her would overhear and turn around and protest. Maybe hand her a magic vial full of cancer-curing-potion. Turn out to be a leprechaun . . . anything. But the time had come to lay the cards out on the table and look them over honestly. She had a losing hand. The only question, really, was how she would handle the tail end of life that fate had left her. And once she asked herself that question, really asked it, like she actually wanted to hear the answer, she found she already knew. Some corner of her mind had worked it all out already and had the plan waiting to whip out and lay down. Maybe it wouldn't have made sense to anyone else. But it made sense to Bea.

The metro had reached the end of the line and turned back around. When it slid to a stop at her home station, Bea stood up and took a long look around. The people seemed so beautiful. She longed to be one of them, to stay on the train. But a line had been drawn that only she could see, and she knew she couldn't hide from it. Not anymore. She had preparations to make, things she needed to do. She sighed once, and then stepped briskly off the train.

BEA

The docks had changed so much it hurt Bea to look at them. In her memory, this was a sun-filled place, full of hot dog stands and voices hollering, of children running back and forth, looking at the ducks. In her memory, her grandfather was there, grumbling and cursing as he pulled the tarp off the boat, watching her sharply as she readied the sail. He was always watching, always ready to yell at her at the slightest mistake. But she rarely made any, and as he watched her, there was quiet satisfaction in his eyes. And if he yelled, his eyes would sparkle with delight if she turned around and yelled right back.

But her grandfather was gone. And the docks were a ruin.

Grimy and deserted, they were the stinking, rotting corpse of her childhood dreams. The one restaurant that wasn't boarded up had left buckets of fish out decaying by the door, and the pavement was stained with blood.

It didn't matter, though. The boat was all that mattered.

When her grandfather had died, Bea's mom had wanted to sell it. She could barely stand to talk to her father while he was alive; now that he was dead, she didn't want to be burdened with the boat that had been his life, his joy. The boat he had openly adored more than he ever adored her. But some residual guilt, some unspoken longing for the father who had neglected her when she was a child, and that she, in turn, had neglected in his old age, kept the boat off the auctioning block. Her mom and dad took it out only once or twice a year. On the fourth of July, to watch the fireworks. On a summer Sunday when they could think of nothing they wanted to do. Bea had never gone with them. She couldn't stand the thought of being on the boat without her grandfather . . . it would be like seeing his ghost.

But now she went to it eagerly, hungrily. Now, she was half-ghost herself.

She could feel it had been waiting for her. The smooth feel of its wood under her hand was a caress, the sway under her feet a small dance of happiness at her return. She remembered this: the wind and the spray and the green water. She craved it, had to have it. No medicine could cure her body, and now the ocean was the only drug that could soothe her soul.

The boat was dusty after years of neglect. She half laughed as she walked the length, imagining how her grandfather would have reacted if he had ever seen it like this. But, though it had been years since she had seen it, she still knew it like it was a part of herself. She knew that it was sturdy and strong under all the dirt. It needed her just as much as she needed it. She smiled as she found a bucket, filled it with water, and scrubbed.

Bea felt her grandfather watching her as she worked; she could hear the echo of his cursing in the wind. He had been a Navy man. Even when the war was over, after he had come home and gotten married, had two daughters and a son . . . the sea had never let him go. He opened a boat-building business with two of his old shipmates. It had done well, had sent his children to the finest private schools, let his wife enjoy the upper social circles. He had hardly seen them. By the time he retired and looked around, actually wanting, for the first time in a long time, to give love and get some in return, his wife was gone and his children hated him.

Not Bea, though. She had his toughness, his strength. His independence. And in an amazingly short time she, too, had his love of the water. He was a patient, though foul-mouthed teacher, and under his careful eye, Bea soon learned how to make herself useful on the boat. Bea also learned to curse from him. It was like a second language they shared; they spoke it fluently and in secret. She used to escape with her grandpa on the boat every weekend. The summer after her twelfth birthday they went on a month-long trip, just the two of them, sailing and fishing and sharing the joy of the wind on their faces. It all came back to her as soon as she was on deck. After a few hours, the memories were more real to her than the whole past year of sickness. The echo of her grandfather's voice was louder, sweeter than anything that called her back to land.

She worked efficiently, despite the discomfort. Moving her arms this way pulled painfully on the wounds on her chest, and she had to keep stopping to catch her breath. The water sloshed in the bucket. Anxiety tugged at her; fear of discovery, worry that someone would see what she was doing, and try to make her stop. She couldn't stop, she knew that now. Knew this was the call tugging inside her, the one she had to answer. She could not work late into the night; she was too smart to stay near the docks when the sun faded. She knew what this neighborhood had become. But her hand caressed the hull before she left, a silent promise of return.

When she walked up to her house in the late twilight, Evie's car was parked back in front of her house. Evie was sitting on the hood. She slid down and stood leaning against the car as Bea got closer.

"I'm sorry about running off," Bea said, before Evie could say anything.

"You don't need to apologize," Evie shrugged. "I'm honestly not even sure what I want to say." She looked Bea in the eye, her eyes shining. "I wish I could do something."

"You've done a lot. I mean it," Bea insisted when she saw Evie shake her head. "You've been a friend, and that's worth a lot. And the way you look at me has never changed, no matter what. And that means the world." Bea hesitated, looking down at the pavement, scuffing the cement with the toe of her shoe. "I love you. You know?"

She was looking down, so she didn't see the hug coming, but a second later, Evie's arms were wrapped around her shoulders in a gentle, warm embrace.

"Love you too," Evie's muffled voice said in her ear.

They parted, Evie looking away as she ran a hand over her eyes, Bea wiping her nose on the sleeve of her jacket.

"I'll come by and see you tomorrow," Evie offered. Bea shook her head.

"I've got stuff going on tomorrow," she said. She couldn't quite meet Evie's eyes.

"The day after, then?"

"Yeah. Sometime real soon. Just call me okay?"

"Sure."

Bea could hear a touch of uncertainty in Evie's voice, so she looked up and smiled.

"Text me if that dude tries to do more than just buy you some cake." She raised her eyebrows suggestively, and Evie laughed, just as she'd hoped.

"Deal. See you soon."

"Yup. Soon."

Bea resisted the desire to stand and watch as Evie's car pulled away. She wrapped her arms tightly around her waist and walked into the house as quickly as she could manage.

She was glad she hadn't missed dinner. That night, she ate at the table with her parents and tried to talk to them as much as she could, tried to shrug off the silence growing inside her one last time. They even laughed a little. She gave them long hugs before they separated for the night, telling them how much she loved them, kissing her surprised father on the cheek.

Was it gentler this way? she wondered, as she quietly shoved her swimsuit and some of her paperback novels into her duffel bag. Was this easier than months spent watching her suffer and splinter and die? Kinder than the white gleam of hospital gowns and the soft smell of chemicals that would linger and grow familiar on their clothes? She hoped so. She honestly hoped it was better this way, for everyone. But she couldn't really know. She just knew it had to be.

When they woke in the morning, she was already gone.

She had written two long e-mails. One to her parents, and one to Evie. But she hadn't sent them yet. She had scheduled them to send in two days. They wouldn't be sure, at first. She had taken hardly any clothes, only a bit of food. She'd brought all her medications.

The feeling she got as the boat pulled out into the water was better than she could have imagined, better than anything. The relief of turning her back on the city, knowing it was fading away into the early morning mist. She went as fast as she could, hurrying, anxious to be far enough away that there would be no other boats, no other eyes. No one but her and the ghost of her grandfather standing, waiting patiently, by her side.

On the morning of the second day she steered the boat east, straight toward the sunset. She pulled her phone out of her pocket and stared at it. There were no little bars there, but she knew that the e-mails had been sent. Knew that, if she had been in range, the phone would have been ringing. She closed her eyes, thinking of the words she had sent them, hoping they were enough to make them understand. "I'm leaving," she had said. "I can't help it. I can't do this anymore . . . I hate it too much. I can't stand to keep trying. I'm sorry. Sorry for leaving you, for running away. So sorry that I ever got sick in the first place. I wish I was strong enough to get better, wish there were some words I could say that would make this not hurt you. I feel like I'll disappear if I keep going . . . like the chemo will burn *me* away, instead of the cancer. I don't know how to stay, how to die this way . . . and still be me. I have to go—please, try to understand. I hope that, someday, you can forgive me. I love you always." The blank face of her phone stared back at her. She would never know what her mom or dad, or Evie, would have said in reply.

Walking over to the side of the boat, she held the phone out over the water and let it slip from her hand. The splash was loud in the morning stillness, a declaration—an offering—though to what or who she was not sure. The mist clung to the surface of the water, kissing her face, hugging her skin. There were no other boats now. No one else, no land, only her and her boat and the water. It was everything she wanted; it was perfection and simplicity and peace.

Next came the pills. She opened the bottles one by one, holding them high in the air, letting the contents spill out slowly, watching them go.

"Enough," she whispered. "No more."

When the pills were gone, she stood silent for a moment, and then, smiling, she pulled off her shirt and threw it to the waves. The wounds were still red and angry. Now she was done hiding them, done enduring the feel of fabric on her skin, when the slightest whisper of a touch was agony. She turned her head to the side so she could see the port that the doctors had installed on her chest. She had dreamed of the day she could have it removed, but now that day would never come. Like the cancer, it would remain, inside her but not a part of her, an unwelcome hitchhiker, clinging to her always. But somehow, with the wind on her face and the sea all around, Bea didn't care. Standing on the deck in just her swimsuit bottom, all she felt was free.

She stretched her hands to the sky, feeling the puckered skin on her chest pulling tight in the sunshine. She was free of it now, free of all of it. Free from pain and fear, and from hope that was continuously disappointed. Even the constant knot of anger that burned and burned deep inside her chest had loosened.

The warm sun pressed against her chest. Bea smiled. There was no reason to hide her scars here. If there was a God, he was the only one watching. And He already knew.

She would sail a little further, she decided. Watch the rest of the sunrise. But she didn't have much farther to go.

She might not be able to escape death, but she damn well could take it by surprise.

MOLLY

Jake slept for three more days. For the first twenty-four hours, Molly sat beside him.

He grumbled in his dreams. He moved, at Molly's urging, from the floor to the bed. But the shaking kept racking him, and sleep kept pulling him back in.

She sat and stared at the closed door. She thought of performing on stage, or her band . . . about every part of her life just a few days ago, and her heart ached with longing. She told herself, over and over again, that what Andrew and the rest of them had said about her could not be true. This world was not where she was meant to be, it was full of people who were broken. Molly was whole. She belonged in the sun.

She told herself that she wasn't staying in the room to avoid seeing Thia, or Andrew, or any of the other Echoes. She definitely was not afraid of facing this new world, or what it might say about her.

She was keeping an eye on Jake. He needed her.

That whole line of thinking felt thin by the second day.

Her stomach rumbled, her head ached. Jake slumbered peacefully, his face so relaxed that it was hard to maintain any pretext about him needing constant watching-over. Time seemed to dig its heels in and slow down. The room was large and full of shadows. Molly was not used to sitting idle, hour after hour. Now she felt caged. Her skin itched. There was no clock, and she didn't know how to measure the passage of time by the passing of the trains overhead. The only way she could find out the time was by picking up Jake's limp wrist and peering at his watch. A little after noon the second day, she realized she had checked Jake's watch three times in less than fifteen minutes.

"Shit," she whispered to herself. "This is ridiculous. *I* am being ridiculous."

She straightened up, pulled away the chair still wedged under the doorknob, and opened the door. A few people were strolling down the hallway past her door, but they didn't stop to give her a second glance. Everyone seemed to go in the same direction. Apparently, Molly wasn't the only one that was hungry.

The tavern seemed like a different place, now that it was filled with people, laughing and jostling and handing around platters of grilled chicken and vegetables. Light flickered from the lanterns that dangled from the ceiling, and the burnished copper pipes that lined the ceiling reflected their glow, filling the whole, wide room with a warm, amber light. The tavern had transformed into a loud, raucous place, where everyone seemed to be yelling and helping themselves to food. They darted behind the bar, filling pitchers with beer or water or lemonade and then carrying them back to the long wooden tables. Molly spotted Thia hard at work behind the bar, a wide grin on her face as she flipped burgers and yelled orders into the back room. Thia glanced up and her smile broadened when she noticed Molly standing, uncertain, in the doorway.

"Grab a seat!" she yelled over the din, gesturing widely, in case Molly couldn't hear her. "I'll bring you something in a sec!"

Molly nodded, glad that at least Thia didn't seem to be holding her earlier, abrupt departure against her.

There were only a few empty spots left in the place, but a small table for two sat empty near the door, and Molly sank down into one of the chairs gratefully. She had barely had time to settle into her seat when Andrew rounded the corner. He smiled when he saw her and didn't wait for an invitation before lowering himself onto the empty seat.

"Hey, Molly," he said, leaning in close to her. A lock of his red hair swung down onto his face, and he swept it behind his ear. "Are you doing okay? I came by your room a few times, but it seemed like you were still resting, and I didn't want to rush you. I know that you've been through a lot."

"I'm fine," Molly said, the lie an instinctive defense.

"I'm glad to hear that," Andrew looked around the room, and Molly could see the pride on his face as his eyes ran over the crowd. "We have such an amazing community here—but I know it's still a lot to take in."

Molly followed his gaze, looking around the room again, with renewed interest. Was she imagining it, or had the atmosphere changed subtly since Andrew's arrival? Everything seemed slightly calmer. Voices still rang out, but the chaos seemed to have calmed down by a couple degrees.

"There he is," Thia crowed, coming up behind Andrew and giving him a brief, tight hug around his shoulders. "I owe you one, Molly, if you're the reason that our fearless leader has ventured out to eat with all the rest of us. It's always a special treat when I get to cook for him!"

"It's always a special treat for me when I get the chance to enjoy your food."

Molly could see how his words made Thia blush happily.

"It isn't often that I can pry myself away from my research. But I'm always happy to be here."

"This man saved my life, did you know that?" Thia asked, patting Andrew on the shoulder as her face flushed with emotion.

"I wouldn't be here today if it weren't for him. And I'd do just about anything for him."

Her voice was thick with sudden emotion, but Andrew smiled easily as he reached over to squeeze her hand.

"Anything?" he asked, his tone light and teasing. "Really? Even making my burger well-done, just the way I like it? Because I seem to remember you giving me a hard time about that before."

Thia closed her eyes and groaned loudly. "Because it's just so *wrong*," she protested. "I want to make you delicious food! Not a hockey puck on a bun. But . . . fine," she shook her head widely as she whipped a small pad of paper out of her pocket and jotted down a note to herself. "One burned, tasteless formerly-known-as-food patty coming right up. But you!" she said, jabbing her pencil in Molly's direction. "You get yours medium-rare. Just like God intended."

Molly laughed. "That sounds perfect," she assured Thia, who was still pouting a little when she turned and trotted back to the kitchen, her ponytail bouncing behind her, to prepare their food.

"I notice that no one else got table-side service and a special menu," Molly observed archly. She wasn't sure how she felt about the way everyone seemed to tiptoe around Andrew, acting as though he was some kind of superhero.

Andrew shrugged. "I guess that being the founder of this place has to come with a few perks."

"You *founded* it?" Molly asked, her voice climbing several octaves.

"Well, I guess 'founding' might make it sound a little too official. More like I was running for my life, stumbled into these abandoned tunnels, and eventually realized that we could actually *do* something with this space. That there could be a place where people like us could be safe." He gestured in the air between them, seeming not to notice how Molly shifted uneasily at the phrase, 'people like us.' "I was just a kid when I first came down here," Andrew explained. "There were enough rumors flying around in my family about odd things happening, an uncle or great aunt one day starting to have everything go their way, and then suddenly disappearing, that I knew what was happening to me when my voice started to surface. Like you, my voice was powerful enough that I got noticed right away. For a long time, I just ran. I was a teenager, alone and clueless. I slept in doorways. I used the power of my voice to keep myself fed, but was too afraid of being discovered to do anything more than get the bare necessities and keep moving on. Then I heard a story about abandoned tunnels, deep under the metro system. I came down here with a friend, and it was like a whole world that was just waiting for us to use it. Once we knew that we had a safe place to disappear to when we needed to, we didn't have to be so careful about not using our voices when we were up on the surface. And we began to build, to make improvements down here. We wanted to make this place really our own, you know? We found more people like us. Eventually, we began actively searching, trying to get to Echoes whose powers had just surfaced before anyone else could."

"Food!" Thia announced as she came to a halt next to their table, and Molly started. Thia slid a plate toward Andrew with a grimace. "Well, in your case, sort-of-food," she corrected herself, and Andrew laughed.

"Thank you," Molly told her, and then shook her head as she had a sudden realization. "You know, I am so sorry! I just realized that I never even paid you for the food I had the other day!" She reached for the bedraggled wallet in her back pocket, even though she was pretty sure that it was more or less bereft of cash. But Thia reached out and stopped her. "No one pays here," she said, patting Molly's hand. "We're all family, here. *Real* family—the kind that actually takes care of each other." The emphasis on her words seemed to imply that she knew plenty about family that didn't take care of each other. Despite herself, Molly felt a deep pang of solidarity. She knew plenty about that kind of family, too. "Well, there you go, guys. Enjoy. I hope you don't want dessert, 'cause I haven't made any. And Matt is crap at baking cakes." Thia winked at them and walked away.

Andrew immediately dug into his burger, and Molly couldn't keep from devouring hers, too. They said hardly a word as they were eating, for which Molly was glad. She was too hungry to worry about niceties like not talking with your mouth full. Besides, she really had no idea what to say.

"Come on back to my office with me for a few minutes," Andrew said when they had both pushed their plates away with a groan. "There are a few things we should talk about in a more private setting." He got up and walked away from the table without waiting for Molly to respond, moving with the air of a person used to being obeyed. Molly hesitated for a minute, then shrugged to herself and got up to walk with him. The truth was, there were plenty of questions she still needed answered. If she could get those answers from him, then she was more than happy to tag along.

She was lost almost instantly in the tangle of hallways and passages, and Andrew pointed at things, trying to give her the lay of the place.

"It isn't as big as it seems at first," he assured her. "It's just the way the tunnels turn in on each other and interconnect that makes things confusing."

Soon they were at the same, metal door that Molly remembered from what seemed like a lifetime ago. Andrew unlocked the door, and Molly stepped inside. Everything was just as she remembered it: the deep leather couches, the small, flickering fire. The walls covered in maps and drawing after drawing of a cup and a knife.

"What are these?" she asked, walking up to a drawing of a large cup done in pen and ink, and running her finger down the paper's surface. "You seem to be . . . um . . . really interested in these things."

"I think the word you're trying to avoid using is 'obsessed'."

Andrew laughed as he threw himself down on one of the couches, stretching his arms back over the sides with a contented sigh. "And you wouldn't be wrong. I'm not ashamed of it. I could never be ashamed of being obsessed with something that is the key to our freedom."

"What do you mean?" Molly asked, settling herself down on the edge of one of the chairs.

"Not that I'm calling our place down here a prison!" Andrew hurried to explain, as though afraid he would offend her, which Molly found just a little bit ironic. "I love it down here. I built this place with my own hands, and I know how important it is. What it means to us. But still, I know things could be different. Better. We shouldn't have to hide or to act as though we are ashamed of what we are and what we can do. And these . . ." Andrew waved a hand at his drawings. "You might not believe me but, someday . . ." he shook his head. "Someday soon, they're going to change everything for us."

"How?" Molly craned her head back around too look at the pictures. "How are an old cup and a . . ." she hesitated for a minute to be sure she was deciphering the drawings correctly. Apparently, Andrew wasn't the best artist in the world. "A knife, going to change everything?"

"These items are relics. Part of Siren . . . and therefore *our* . . . history. The stories behind them are long and probably not that interesting to you. Hell, they aren't that interesting to me! What matters is that we know they're imbued with power."

Molly raised an eyebrow and Andrew chuckled at her skeptical expression. "Really. All the accounts agree on that. The number of scrolls that exist about these things: describing them, singing songs about them, giving long, boring warnings regarding them. You wouldn't believe it, Molly! They're real. As real as you and me. As real as the power that we hold inside us."

Molly didn't like the way he kept speaking as though they were the same, and she didn't like the way his voice was making her lean forward in her seat, or the fact that she found it so difficult to tear her eyes from his.

"We don't need the knife," Andrew went on, "but it's still important because it and the goblet have traveled together through history. Find one, and you'll find the other. And the goblet is what we need." He got up and walked in long, eager strides, over to the wall. He unpinned one of the drawings of the goblet and looked at it for a long, silent moment, before turning and coming to sit back down across from Molly, the picture still clutched tightly in his hand. "The goblet is the key. If we had it, we wouldn't have to hide down here in the dark anymore." He leaned forward, pushing his hair back from his forehead and resting his elbows on his knees. "If someone like us—with both human and Siren blood—drinks from this goblet, their voice changes. They would become just as powerful as the full-blooded Sirens."

Molly sucked in a deep breath of surprise. If Andrew was right, then he hadn't been exaggerating when he had said that what he was searching for could change the world.

"Imagine it, Molly!" he said, his eyes a little unfocused. He smiled, his eyes looking over Molly's shoulder, as though he could actually see the future he was describing with so much fervor. "We wouldn't have to be afraid of the Legacies, or even of the Sirens themselves. We could come out of the tunnels, out of the shadows. We could have the place in the world that ought to be ours already." The elation on his face drained away as suddenly as it had come. He sat back in his chair and tightened his fist, crushing the drawing in his hand into a tight ball. "*IF* I could find the damn thing." Andrew threw the ruined paper onto the floor, and rubbed his forehead roughly with the palms of his hands. "I've been searching for years and years. I thought Evie would finally solve the puzzle for me, but all she found were more dead-ends." He laughed ruefully. "I feel like I've been staring at the same damn puzzle pieces for years, always on the verge of figuring out how they fit together, but never quite able to make it work. But now . .

." his lips turned up at the corners, and a smile began to slowly reappear on his face. "Now that I've found *you*, I feel like I have a crucial piece of the puzzle that I never had before."

"Me?" Molly's voice climbed several octaves in her surprise. "What have I got to do with any of this?"

Andrew grinned sheepishly. "Well, I really didn't want to spring too much of this on you at once. But here's the thing Molly: your voice is powerful. Truly, deeply powerful." Molly shook her head in automatic denial, but Andrew took no notice. "I'm not saying that, once you're trained up, you'll be more powerful than me." Andrew gave her an appraising look. "But if my guess is right, you'll come pretty damn close. But the thing that matters most, Molly, is that each person's gift is unique. They've each got their own little twist, or quirk. And after watching you sing in the bar the other night, I know what yours is already."

"You do?" Molly couldn't stop herself from asking, "What is it?"

Andrew smiled broadly. "You can use your voice to control a whole group of people at once. A large group of people, even. Do you have any idea how difficult that is?" Andrew gave a low whistle. "If I hadn't seen you do it, I would have said it was impossible. But here you sit." He gestured in her direction.

"I don't understand. What does that have to do with the goblet?"

"Do you think they leave that thing unguarded?" Andrew cried, his eyebrows rising almost to his hairline. "They may be bloodthirsty, cruel, insane monsters drunk on their own power . . . but they aren't stupid. Once we find the goblet, then we actually have to get to it."

"Wait a minute," Molly cried, finally catching her breath enough to break in. "I haven't agreed to any of this, and I honestly don't believe half the things you're saying and . . ."

"I'm sorry, I've gotten way ahead of myself," Andrew cut her off with a wave and a smile. "There's no reason to start worrying about all this stuff now. There's something else I need to talk to you about. It has to do with your friend. Jake."

All thoughts of a goblet or a crazy, mythology-fueled crusade fled Molly's mind in an instant.

"What about Jake?" she asked. Something about Andrew's expression made her chest tight. Her fingertips suddenly felt cold.

"Well, speaking of your unusually strong abilities, I feel like I have to say this." Andrew folded his hands in front of him and stared down at his fingers. "What happened to Jake . . . the way that you bound him to you. You didn't know what you were doing. There are some powerful instincts inside you that are just now starting to surface. That whole situation should never have happened. It was an accident, and I don't want you to feel . . . obligated . . . to that person. To Jake. I could help you, if you wanted, could do things to make it easier on him. Without burdening you."

"No." Molly said, shaking her head, trying not to sound frantic. "We're fine."

The thought of being separated from Jake filled her with a sharp, aching dread. He was the only person in this whole dark, underground world who she really trusted. The way he had wrapped his arms around her and told her she wasn't alone. The thought of losing that, or losing him, was too painful to even think of.

"Molly . . ." Andrew hesitated, seeming to choose his words with care. "I know that right now it feels like you can do anything at all, anything you want. But there are limits. I don't want you to get in over your head when you're just learning how this works. I can help you . . ."

"Jake stays with me." Molly bit out the words. She felt anger rising, and she didn't try to keep it from burning in her eyes. If Andrew tried to do anything to get between her and Jake, he was in for a fight. She wanted him to know that right from the start.

"Alright," Andrew said uncertainly. "If you're sure."

Molly gave him a tight-lipped smile. "I am."

"Okay, then I need to mention something else." Andrew cleared his throat, and Molly wondered, in the back of her mind, how often people told Andrew 'No.' She was willing to bet that it was a word he didn't hear often. "What happened with Jake attracted a lot of attention to you. People here are talking. Most of the Echoes here aren't strong enough to claim a Bloodbound at all, and you did it on your first night. Having a Bloodbound is a kind of status symbol here."

"Jake is NOT a status symbol," Molly cut in sharply. "He's a person."

"Be that as it may," Andrew's eyes hardened, and suddenly, Molly remembered that she ought to be cautious. Andrew had already proved to her he could use his voice to force her to do things against her will—and that he apparently had no qualms about doing just that. Making him angry could be very dangerous . . . both for her, and for Jake. "There may be people who feel . . . threatened by you. They may feel the need to prove that, despite your impressive arrival, they are still more powerful than you are. Usually, a newbie gets a few weeks' grace before people start to challenge her. For you, after what's happened, it may be less."

"Challenge me how?"

"We all have ranks here. I, obviously, am on the top. Tyler is my second. From us, it stretches down all the way to the bottom. You move up on the ladder by challenging the person above you to a match. If you win, you take that person's spot, and they move down a rung on the ladder. Now, matches here are usually pretty simple. You try to use your voice to force another Echo to do your bidding. Sometimes it's only for a second, but as long as you prove that you can overcome them, it's enough. Toward the bottom, the matches are pretty minor. Someone will try to make you punch yourself in the face, tie your own shoelaces together . . . goofing around." Andrew shrugged indulgently. "But once you get to the top, it's serious. The matches can be deadly. I want you to be very, very careful. Keep your head down until you've really got a handle on your ability. Try not to piss anybody off too badly. I don't want you putting yourself at risk."

"Sure," Molly said. "I guess that makes sense."

"Good," Andrew nodded. "And I'm going to work one on one with you, to get you up to speed as quickly as possible. Usually, we have a trainer who works with our 'new recruits.' But I want to train you myself." He stood up and walked toward the door. Molly, realizing that their conversation was over, jumped to her feet. She was happy to get out of that room. Her head was aching with all the new information she needed to think through and sort out. And she wanted to check on Jake.

"Be back here, bright and early tomorrow morning," Andrew told her as he opened the door. "We'll eat breakfast together, and get right back to work."

Jake was still sleeping when Molly got back to the room. She watched him closely; it didn't look like he had moved all day. She adjusted his blanket and tried to fight back panic. Wouldn't he need an IV, or something, if he slept much longer? How much longer could he go without fluids? Had she accidentally put him into a coma? She sat beside him for a while, watching the slow rise and fall of his chest, studying the off-white pallor of his skin, stroking his bristly hair. Finally, she could think of nothing to do but crawl into bed beside him. The steady in and out of his breathing was more calming than a sedative and, before she knew it, Molly was slipping into dreams.

The next morning, he was still hadn't woken. *If he's still sleeping when I come back this afternoon, I'll have Matt come and check on him,* she promised herself. *He can't go on like this much longer.*

She feared getting lost in the tunnels, but after just one false turn, she found herself standing in front of Andrew's door. She knocked, and a woman answered. Molly tried to keep the surprise from showing in her eyes. She hadn't realized that Andrew had a .

. . companion. The beautiful woman with thick black hair hanging down to her waist held the door open just far enough for her eyes to run up and down Molly.

"Can I help you?" she asked, something in her tone implying that she suspected that Molly needed lots of help, but that she wasn't especially interested in providing it.

"Um, Andrew told me to come see him?" Molly said, realizing as she spoke she had made her words a question. The woman seemed half determined to prevent her from entering Andrew's rooms, and Molly was more than willing to let her.

"Wait," the woman said, closing the door right in Molly's face. But before Molly could feel anything but surprise, the door reopened, and the woman nodded to her coolly.

"Come in," she said, her voice devoid of any emotion, somehow reminding Molly of the computerized voice on a phone answering system.

Molly got a better look at the woman as she entered the room. Taller than Molly, with perfectly straight hair that swung thickly down to her hips, she was curvy and slender at the same time. She wore a sleeveless black dress that plummeted at the neckline and stopped above the knee. Around her wrist she wore a bracelet of blood-red stones.

Whatever Molly had been expecting when Andrew told her to come to his room for breakfast and training, it wasn't what she found. His table was piled high with plates crowded with omelets and trays of hash browns. Strong black coffee and sliced fruit. Andrew was already sitting at the table, elbow deep in a plate with scrambled eggs.

"Come on in!" He encouraged her around a mouth full of food. "Denise really out-did herself this time." At his gesture, Molly took the empty seat across from him. Andrew turned to the woman. "Denise, sweetheart, thanks again. Everything is delicious. Why don't you give Molly and I some privacy now?"

The woman nodded, the movement seeming a little jerky to Molly, and walked, somewhat unsteadily, from the room.

"Dig in!" Andrew encouraged her, and handed Molly an over-full plate. Andrew finished his food and then sipped his coffee, smiling as he watched her shovel it in.

"Sorry," she said, setting her fork down after what she knew to be a long silence. "I didn't mean to sit and stuff my face. That food was really good."

"I wish I could take the credit, but that's Denise's work. Not to denigrate Thia's cooking at all, but she does tend to stick with what she knows. Even *her* burgers can get old, after a while. So," he set his coffee cup down on the table, "now that you've eaten, I think that it's time for us to begin."

"Okay . . ." Molly answered uncertainly, a sudden swooping feeling in her stomach.

"Don't be nervous!" Andrew urged her. "Just come stand across from me."

She dragged her feet as she joined him, standing beside one of his couches.

"Spread your feet shoulder length apart," Andrew instructed. "Good. Just like that. Close your eyes."

Molly did as he instructed, even though a part of her didn't like the feeling of vulnerability that came with having her eyes closed.

"Now," Andrew's deep, velvety voice said, "I want you to give me an order."

"An order?" Molly shifted her weight uncomfortably from one foot to the other.

"Yes. It can be for anything. You can order me to sit down, or hop on one foot." Andrew chuckled. "Don't worry, I won't have any trouble refusing if I want to. This is just for practice. Like sparring. You can practice giving commands, and I'll start to show you how to resist them, too. The skills are related. Anyway, just go for it. I'm ready."

Molly hesitated for a minute, wondering if there was any way in the world she could get out of this situation. Nothing sprang to mind.

"Sit down," she told Andrew half-heartedly.

He laughed. "Oh, come on," he urged her. "I know you can do better than that."

The day went downhill from there. After spending a long time trying to get Molly to use the power of her voice, with absolutely no success, Andrew switched tracks. He gave her commands, urging her to push away the pull of his words. He gave her harmless orders, telling her to sit down, stand up, or sneeze on command.

But Molly didn't like it.

Each time her body moved without her permission, she fought and fought as hard as she could. It didn't make the slightest bit of difference. Her head pounded. Her body grew sweaty and shaky and, no matter what she did, she followed each and every one of Andrew's command. Finally, when she bit down on her own lip so hard that it bled, trying and failing to resist the command that Andrew gave her to say 'Uncle,' Molly couldn't stomach anymore.

"I'm done with this," she spat, wiping a trickle of blood from her chin. Andrew's eyes had lost their sparkle as he nodded his assent.

"Fine," he agreed, "there's no point in carrying on like this. But we'll start again, first thing in the morning."

"What is the point?" Molly cried, clutching her aching head in her hands. "I can't do this—I don't want to do this. I have no idea what you even want from me right now."

"I want you to stop hiding your strength," Andrew snapped.

"I'm not hiding anything!" Molly protested. "I've told you over and over again: I'm not one of you."

"Whether you are hiding your power, or hiding *from* it makes no difference." Andrew cried, his temper flashing in his eyes. "The ability is inside you. I've seen you use it; I've heard it with my own ears. It will surface. It must."

Molly turned on her heel and strode toward the door. "I have to go now. I need to check on Jake." She half expected Andrew to force her to stay. But he remained a silent, glowering presence behind her as Molly stepped out into the hallway, and slammed the door.

Her anger with Andrew faded quickly, swallowed up by her growing worry for Jake. She rushed back to their room. *I'll have to find Matt, if Jake's still sleeping,* she told herself. *He can't go on like this much longer.*

She pushed the door open, and relief flooded her. "Jake!"

"Hi." Jake jumped up when she entered, looking at her intently for a second before dropping his eyes. He looked . . . better. His skin was still pale, and he had the gaunt, lean look of someone who had lost weight too quickly. But he had shaved the stubble from his chin, and his face was clean. His worn, dirty, clothes had been replaced with a crisp black shirt and black jeans. He had a bracelet of red beads wrapped around his wrist.

"I was so worried about you!" Molly cried, taking an eager step toward him before catching herself. In an instant, her relief evaporated. She realized that she had no idea how Jake felt toward her now. Would he resent the bond she had created between them? Would he be angry with her? Or even fear her? She didn't know if she could bear it if he turned away from her now. She had touched his cheek so many times while he was sleeping. Now she missed the rough feeling of his face on her fingertips. Hardly knowing what to do with herself, Molly side-stepped to the bed and settled herself down cross-legged on top of it. Jake wouldn't meet her eyes. Her heart ached.

"How is your hand feeling?" she asked, and breathed deeply with relief when he looked up at her and smiled.

"It doesn't hurt at all." Jake held his hand up for her to see. It was wrapped tightly with gauze. "I found that medic again today."

"Matt?"

"That's right. He changed the bandage for me, then took me to Thia. She got me all set up."

"I'm so sorry I wasn't here when you woke up. Are you hungry? Have you eaten? What do you need?"

"Please, don't worry about it." Jake came and sat down on the floor in front of the bed, pulling his knees up to his chest and gazing at her. "I can take care of myself. I don't want you to go to any trouble for me . . . it should be the other way around. Thia helped me get food, and clothes, and blankets." He nodded to a makeshift bed he had laid out for himself against the far wall of the room, and Molly felt a pang of regret. She had liked the warmth of having him in bed beside her. "She showed me around a little, told me how things work here. And she gave me this."

He held up his wrist and the tiny red links that glinted there. It looked just like the one she had noticed Denise wearing this morning. Several things fell into place in Molly's mind.

Bloodbound.

That's what they called . . . what he was. Suddenly, Molly understood the significance of the bracelet.

"You don't have to wear that, Jake," she told him quickly, leaning forward on the bed.

"Why shouldn't I?" Jake answered. He looked right at her, his dark eyes burning. "Do you think I'm embarrassed to belong to you?" He shook his head forcefully. "I'm not."

Molly had no idea how to respond to that, so she changed the subject. "I like your clothes," she commented. "They suit you. You really look a lot better."

"I feel a lot better," Jake said softly. "Thanks to you."

"Is there anything else you need, Jake? Anything you want?"

Jake hesitated. "Don't ask me that," he said, looking away.

"Why not? I want to do everything I can for you. I want to know what you need." She leaned over so she could touch his shoulder gently.

"You might not like the answer."

"I still want to hear it. Tell me."

"I want you," Jake admitted in a rush, the words spilling out. He looked up at her, his eyes wide, afraid of her reaction. "I mean, I know it wouldn't be . . . I mean, I know I'm not . . ." His words trailed off, and he looked away. "I just want to be close to you, Molly. You've always been so amazing to me. Those nights, talking to you in the bar." Jake swallowed noisily. "They were the best nights of my life. And you knew . . . you knew about me." He gestured to the needle marks that covered his forearms like constellations of stars. "But it never changed the way you looked at me. You talked to me like I was a whole person. Even though I'm not—and haven't been in a long time. And you always listened so carefully to everything I said. You even laughed at my jokes." He winced, as though the memory was a painful one. His voice grew husky. "I want more of that. I want to be close to you. I don't expect for it to last. Even if it's just for a minute." He closed his eyes, as though he couldn't bear to look at her.

Molly slid off the bed and knelt in front of him. She ran her fingers through the soft, short hair on his head. He gasped when she touched him, tilting his head to rest against her hand. She pulled his bandaged hand to her lips. She stroked his cheek.

Leaning in, she kissed him.

Jake moaned, and his fingers fisted in her hair. His lips parted. Their kiss deepened. Molly's head spun, and she felt as though she was falling into him, her whole being pulled in and swallowed up by the depth of his need. He lay his hands against her cheeks, cradling her face with such tenderness that tears sprang to her eyes. There was no feeling in the world like being wanted this much. No high that could compare to having someone else *need* you this deeply, or to the thrill of giving yourself over to their need.

"It's been a long time since I did this," Molly murmured as he kissed her neck. "I'm not sure . . ."

"We'll go as slow as you want," Jake whispered in her ear. "I'll do anything you want."

His lips found hers again, his arms clutching her tight. Molly stiffened for a second, then melted into his embrace, as a delightful sensation she had not felt for a very, very long time rushed through her.

She had worried this part of her was broken. She had been afraid that, when she buried her past, a part of her had been lost beyond reclaiming. But when Jake touched her, her body warmed until it burned. Molly closed her eyes. She could have sworn that her whole body pulsated with light.

"Not too slow," she whispered. "Take off your shirt."

Jake ripped his shirt from his back. She ran her fingers across his smooth skin, through the curled hair on his chest.

"Are you sure?" she asked a minute later, her lips pressing against his earlobe, where her teeth had left their mark. "You don't have to."

"Please," he whispered.

So Molly mounted him, and loved him, and pulled him inside her. When it was over, they lay in a tangle, her head on his chest.

"Now you really are mine," she murmured.

"Forever," Jake agreed.

JAKE

Jake's world had shrunk. He lay in the dark with his arms wrapped around Molly as she slept, memories stinging him like bees. The images of him holding a knife, attacking her, aiming for her heart, flashed, razor sharp, through his mind one after the other. Everything else felt insubstantial and paper thin. He remembered Molly's concerts, though. Her music still swam in his head, her songs the secret soundtrack of his life. He had always wanted her. But he was a junkie and a loser, and he never tried to push knowing her past. He felt lucky to talk to her after the show sometimes.

The idea that she seemed to want him with her now, that she had so effortlessly forgiven him for the damage he did her, he didn't quite understand.

When she had walked into the bedroom earlier, he had half expected her to spit in his face, to use the irresistible power that she suddenly had over him to take some kind of revenge for the harm he had done her. The damage to his hand didn't count for anything. He had struck first, attacked her with a knife while her hands strained against the ropes, keeping them in place behind her back. She had acted in pure self-defense.

He wouldn't have blamed her for killing him.

Instead, she had helped him. She had taken away his pain, kept him close. Insisted that the leader here not do the smart thing and throw him back out on the street.

Jake stretched out his legs, careful not to let the movement disturb Molly. He rolled his head from side to side on the pillow, feeling his bones creak. Everything felt so strange. Disconnected.

She had told him not to feel any pain, and his body seemed to obey her, more or less. It was easier now that she was here, and he could hold onto her, cling to her like an anchor. His hand didn't hurt. His veins didn't burn. But when he woke in an empty room, with Molly nowhere in sight, the first thing he wanted was drugs.

The craving wasn't gone. It was just curled up inside him: a long, venomous snake twisted around Jake's innards, fangs bared, a hiss of need deep inside him that hummed and throbbed. It was different than it had been before, but he was far from cured. Jake closed his eyes. He knew perfectly well there were two halves of his addiction: the pain of need in his body, and the soul-deep craving in his mind and heart. Molly had quieted the pain, had put his body to sleep better than the world's best pain-killer. But even her voice couldn't slay the beast he had long ago invited to take up residence inside him.

The drugs still owned him. There was no way this could last.

But what a lovely interlude, he thought, burying his nose in Molly's hair and breathing in the scent of her. The feel of her skin under his fingers was silk; her hair smelled like honey. Who would have thought he would get to have this brief reprieve before he ended up face down in some gutter? Every moment that he spent with Molly was like a dream. True, the dream was shot through with streaks of pain, fear, and confusion—but it was still better than anything that he'd had in years; worlds better than anything he could have imagined for himself, or felt he deserved.

He would take it, and be grateful. Every moment that he could steal with Molly, every day he could manage to be by her side was a gift the universe never should have trusted him with. He would pocket as many of those moments as he could.

Molly stirred, stretching luxuriously, her bare flesh brushing against his in all kinds of interesting places. Her eyes were still foggy with sleep when she woke and smiled at him, a few strands of hair spilling over her face.

"Good morning," she murmured, her voice a little gravelly. Jake's heart stirred at the sound. Her brow wrinkled. "Or is it afternoon? I think I've lost track of time a little."

"I'm not sure," he whispered, running his fingers down the small of her back. To his delight, she closed her eyes with pleasure and arched her body toward his touch. "I've been a little distracted."

"Hmmm," she sighed. "Do you want to go get something to eat?"

"I want to do whatever you want," he told her, his fingers continuing to explore under the sheets. "What do *you* want, Molly?"

She opened her eyes, and they were dark pools of shining amber.

"You," She answered simply, and put her hands on either side of his head, pulling him to her, letting her teeth sink down on his lower lip. Jake's heart sped up, his blood surged, and he pressed himself against her with desperate fervor.

"MOLLY!" There was a scream from the hallway, and then someone was banging frantically against their door. "Molly! Are you in there?"

Molly turned her head to the door, her eyes wide. "What is it?" she cried. "Who's there?"

"It's Thia!" the voice called back, though Jake would have never guessed that the cracked, panicked voice that came through the door belonged to the funny, self-assured woman he remembered from the day before. "Come on!" she screamed. "Right the fuck now! We're under attack! Steele's here —he's found the

Refuge. We've got to run right now, or we're all going to *fucking* die!"

Jake's eyes locked with Molly's. There was a second of perfect understanding and agreement between them.

Then they moved.

Molly rolled out of bed, her body turning with sinuous grace that, even in his haste, Jake noted and appreciated. He picked her shirt up off the floor and tossed it to her before grabbing his jeans and yanking them on.

Just then an alarm sounded: a deep, low, pulsing cry that emanated from somewhere far down the hall. Now that he was listening for it, Jake could hear feet pounding in the distance. He thought he heard a woman scream.

"We're coming!" Molly yelled over the din, as Jake pulled his tee shirt back over his head.

He noticed that, even as she hurried, Molly took a second to pick up the two thick bracelets she always wore, and slip them back onto her forearm. Then she threw the door open. Thia was practically hopping up and down as she waited, and as soon as the door opened she grabbed Molly by the wrist.

"We've got to go. NOW," she said, glancing over to Jake. "Matt's getting our key."

Then, still holding onto Molly's wrist, she ran. Jake jogged behind them. The alarm still blaring in the background was so loud that it made Jake's head pound. He could hear thumps, bangs, and sometimes feet running. But no one called out. He caught a glimpse of a few people running together in the opposite direction, but they didn't stop to look at their little group, and Thia ignored them.

"What do you mean, getting a key?" Jake called out to Thia. He didn't quite trust this woman, whose eyes were wide with fear, to know how to get them to safety. And she wasn't taking them toward the elevator, which seemed to be the place they should be going if they needed to get out.

"The evacuation plan," she called over her shoulder, her feet never slowing "You haven't been down here long enough to know about it. There are safe rooms all over the city. If the Refuge is compromised, each team grabs a key to one of the rooms and runs for it. I figured since you guys hadn't been assigned a team yet, I'd come and get you."

"Your team is just you and Matt?" Molly gasped, a little out of breath from running.

"Shelia and Chris were on our team too," Thia answered without looking at her. "But when I got to their room they were already dead."

Holy fuck.

Jake's breath caught in his throat. Molly looked back at him, and he saw when the fear hit her. Her eyes widened, and her face went pale. They were in way over their heads with this shit. He had no freaking clue what was going on right now. But getting the hell out of dodge seemed like a pretty good idea.

"How much farther?" Molly asked. She reached out and caught Jake's hand in hers. "Where's Matt?"

"There," Thia pointed, as they rounded a corner. Matt stood with a flashlight behind a panel of wall he pushed aside, reaching out—beckoning—for them to hurry. His forehead was sweaty and his too-long hair clung to the side of his face.

"Come on," Matt called to them, his voice a harsh whisper. "Hurry up. They're close."

Jake didn't know who 'they' were, but from the expression on Matt's face, he was sure that he didn't want to find out. One after another, they stepped into darkness, and Matt grunted as he pulled the panel back into place.

A second later, they were standing in a dark, narrow passage inside the wall. The only light was the flashlight Matt held, and it vibrated with the slight tremor of his hand. In the distance, Jake could see the faint glimmer of light that seemed to leak in from a grate in the wall. Matt held the light up so they could see him. His face was sickly pale and ghostlike in the yellow light.

"The walls are very thin here," he whispered. "So don't make any noise until we're out in the tunnels, okay? We don't want them to hear us."

They all nodded their assent, and Matt turned and walked slowly, leading the way. The pavement beneath their feet was cracked and uneven; and despite Jake's desire to break out into a run, they had to inch along in a cautious, single file line, running their hands against the wall on either side to catch themselves if they stumbled.

There was a large grate in the wall, and as they got closer to it, light and noise leaked through from the other side. Jake could hear a faint voice, and see shadows moving on the other side. Matt bent low and tiptoed past it, and Thia followed suit. But Molly stopped, her eyes peering through the opening. Jake stilled beside her and did the same.

"Come on!" Thia hissed, motioning to them to hurry. But they couldn't move. They both just had to see, to catch a glimpse of what exactly they were running from.

The slats of the iron grate were close together, and it was difficult to see much of anything at first. But after a second, Jake's eyes adjusted. He looked out into a broad hallway. He saw lights flickering. Smoke, or maybe it was steam, floated through the air.

Bodies lay on the ground.

Jake's heart stuttered, and for a second he hoped he was wrong. Maybe those motionless forms were just knocked out. Maybe they were hurt, but still breathing. But he had seen death more than once before, and he knew what it looked like; eyes staring at nothing would never blink and come back into focus again. There were at least three dead on the ground. One was still moving: a woman whose mouth gaped open and shut, silent, like a fish out of water.

Jake's breath caught in his throat, and the blessed detachment of shock floated through him, like dew settling against his skin.

People were standing around, their backs turned toward him. They seemed to be waiting for something.

Then a new figure strode into sight.

Jake knew, with sudden, bone-deep certainty, this was the man to fear. He moved with casual disregard for the dead and the dying at his feet, a look of mild boredom creasing his face.

The figure was short compared to the other men in the hallway, but somehow he still towered over them, and they all backed up a little, seeming to hunch over into themselves when he drew near. He had wide shoulders and a muscular build, his straight black hair hung down to his unshaven chin. It was only when he was close enough for his men to cower before him that Jake noticed what should have been obvious from the first moment: there was metal embedded deep in the man's throat —plates that seemed implanted in his skin. The steel plates gleamed dangerously in the hallway's flickering light. Jake knew instantly this was the man they were running from and, seeing the cruel glint of his eyes, Jake understood why.

"Let me look at him," Steele ordered. Feet scuffled, and two men pulled a third man out of a shadows, and forced him to stand, trembling, in front of Steele.

"I need Andrew," Steele said, his eyes flickering to the terrified prisoner. "He has property of mine and information I want. Where is he?"

"I don't know," the man gasped. He held out his hands, palms up, in a silent plea for mercy. "I swear I don't."

Steele sighed. He brought a hand up and tapped the side of his neck. Jake thought he heard a faint humming sound.

"TELL ME!" Steele's voice was no louder than it had been a moment before, but the force of it blew through the air, slamming through the walls. Jake felt his teeth chatter with it. The hairs on

the back of his neck stood up, his whole body creeping with a sensation of power akin to an electric shock.

The unfortunate man caught the brunt of it, and he fell to the ground, a sob ripping from him.

"I don't know!" he cried again, though this time the words were a scream.

"Fine then. You're useless," Steele muttered. His fingers brushed at his neck again, and this time Jake did not doubt he heard a mechanical hum echoing lightly in the hallway. ***"DIE."***

The man fell backwards when the words hit him. Jake could see his eyes. His irises burst, red bleeding into blue, clouding over white. It was as though his brain had imploded. His body jerked once, so hard Jake thought he heard a bone crack. Then he went utterly, eternally, still.

Fear like he had never felt it before in his life coursed through him. Jake did not look through the grate anymore. He grabbed hold of Molly's hand and felt the terror radiating through her.

"You've got to come on!" Matt whispered urgently, reaching with fingers outstretched as though he could simply drag the two of them to safety.

Far above, the late train clattered over them. The ceiling vibrated, the noise just enough to hide the sound of their footsteps.

They turned and ran down the tunnel as fast as they could.

The passageway was so dark that Jake soon lost all sense of time and direction. Sweat poured down his face as legs that, for years, had done little more than propel him from one fix to another, strained to move fast enough to get to safety. For what felt like an eternity, he and Molly held onto each other and followed the weak, bobbing light of Matt's flashlight deeper and deeper into the underground maze.

After a while, Jake began to notice a change in the quality of darkness around them. It lightened, almost imperceptibly at first, but soon he knew for certain the black was melting into gray.

Matt stopped short before a metal door. Weak yellow light leaked around the door's edges and spilled into the hallway once Matt managed to coax the door open. The door's hinges protested at the movement with a low creak that seemed hideously noisy to Jake.

"This way," Matt whispered to them, glancing over his shoulder. "We're almost there." Then he stepped into the light. The rest of them followed, hunching their shoulders, feeling exposed and vulnerable out in the open.

"Where are we?" Molly hissed, moving to stand close against the wall. The corridor they had entered was little more than gray cement walls and gravel underfoot, but Jake felt almost sure that they were closer to the surface than they had been not long ago. The air smelled different, like fetid water and gasoline. And it was warmer.

Matt pulled a crumpled piece of paper out of his pocket and smoothed the page out with shaking hands. "We practiced for this," he said. "We had an evacuation plan for if the Refuge was ever compromised. Every team had a set of instructions and a key." He ran the back of his hand over his eyes. "The safe room we were assigned to isn't much further. We'll go there and hide out for a bit. Then we'll make contact. Get instructions on what to do next."

Silently, Thia moved closer to Matt and leaned her head against his shoulder. He wrapped an arm around her and leaned his chin down to rest against the top of her head. "It'll be alright," he told her softly, and Jake suddenly felt like an intruder. Thia's shoulders were shaking. "Everyone knew what to do. Everybody had a safe place to run to. Most of them will have made it out. We have to believe that."

Thia nodded into his shoulder. "What about us?" she asked, her voice muffled. "We have so far to go."

Matt smiled, and somehow the expression didn't look out of place, even though his eyes were tired and his face stained with dirt. "Us?" he asked. "Don't worry about us. A few more steps and we'll be safe in the Fire Swamp!"

Thia choked out a laugh and looked up at him, shaking her head. "Matt!" she cried, her voice a little watery. "Now isn't the time for Princess Bride quotes."

"Ah, that's where you're wrong," he responded, wiping a tear from her cheek. "It's always the right time for a Princess Bride quote. You guys doing okay?" He looked up at Jake and Molly, who nodded uncertainly. "Okay, then let's keep moving."

NO ONE ARGUED. They moved cautiously, glancing over their shoulders and keeping close to the wall, staying as hidden in the shadows as they could.

Jake took slow, deep breaths in through his teeth and tried to keep from wheezing. His chest was painfully tight, his head throbbing. He felt unsteady and kept his eyes down, planting one foot carefully in front of the other, trying not to fall. He didn't even notice anything strange about the walls around them until he heard Molly gasp.

His head snapped up and his feet stilled.

"What is this?" Molly whispered, a mixture of awe and horror in her voice.

Thia glanced at the wall. "Lena," she said simply. "She lives down here—her and some older guy. She's a recluse. Didn't want to stay in the Refuge after Andrew walked her out of the psych ward."

"She lives here?" Jake asked, looking around them at the cement walls and hard gravely ground.

Thia shrugged. "She says she likes it. She has lots of time alone with her murals."

Jake couldn't stop looking at the art painted on the wall's bare face; huge works that spread from floor to ceiling. In some places, it was just incredibly intricate patterns of shapes and colors.

People with hallow eyes strode through hallways that shimmered like diamonds. Business men sat on phantom metro trains that flew through vivid black, seemingly unperturbed by the fact that the flesh on their faces was curling back to reveal bone as white as snow. A dark figure, its face hidden by the shroud it wore, reached out toward Jake, its hands full of fire.

"We've got to keep moving," Molly whispered, pulling gently at his hand. Jake started. He hadn't even realized that he'd been standing motionless, staring at the painting while Matt and Thia moved ahead. He nodded his agreement, but it was still another moment before he could force his feet to move. He could have stared at the paintings for hours.

A part of him wanted to reach out and clasp his hand tight against that proffered fist of churning flame.

The night air stung like needles against his skin when they finally got above ground. Molly looked pale and frightened in the moonlight, and all four put their heads down and ran, moving across a wide open, grassy field with the same distraught feeling mice must have when scampering away from a swooping bird of prey. A huge building loomed in front of them. Jake couldn't see it clearly in the gloom, but there were carefully manicured bushes, and pristine stairs leading to tall pillars of muted white. Matt led them away from the darkened glass doors in the front, and around the back to a sort of loading area. There were dumpsters and empty pallets. And a small, forgotten door in the back of the building.

It didn't look like anything special until they were standing right in front of it but once they were close enough, Jake could see the door made of thick, sturdy metal and it fit, airtight, into the wall around it.

Matt pulled a key out of his pocket, inserted it into the keyhole, and turned. There was a moment of silence, and then a low, drawn out click, followed quickly by another, and another, as a series of locks slid open to let them in. Even after the door was unlocked, it was so heavy that Jake and Molly both had to help Matt pull it open. It made a scraping sound against the ground that seemed thunderous in the silent dark.

They all darted inside, and together they pulled it shut behind them. Matt carefully turned the key again and locked the door behind them. Then they all stood in the small, dark staircase, leaned against the walls, and breathed deep breaths of relief.

"We made it," Thia choked out, leaning her head down and covering her face with her hands. "I was so sure that we were all going to die back there."

"Where's the safe room?" Molly asked, and Matt jerked his head up the stairs. "It's in the attic. It's about twelve flights up. No elevator, but once we're there, we should find emergency food supplies. Blankets, everything we need. We can camp out for a day or so until we can connect back with everybody else."

"What is this place?" Jake asked, looking around him to find some kind of clue. But the walls around him were nondescript.

"A library," Matt told him as he turned and began to wearily lead them up the stairs. "It's closed now, so we don't have to worry about anyone hearing us. During the day we'll just have to make sure not to make any noise that might attract attention."

They climbed the stairs, their feet dragging with exhaustion. Flight after flight, their steps were slow and plodding, echoing in the silence that loomed around them. After what seemed like forever, a door came into view.

Then Jake felt the hairs on the back of his neck stand up.

"Matt!" he whispered urgently. "Are there supposed to be *lights* on in the safe room?"

They all froze; the air seemed to snap with sudden tension around them. They gazed at the telltale line of yellow light streaming beneath the door.

"Someone's in there," Molly murmured, her voice so low now that it was barely audible.

"Maybe another team was assigned the same safe room?" Thia asked, but she didn't sound hopeful.

Matt shook his head sharply. "Couldn't be that," he whispered back. "Andrew was very clear. Each team got their own, separate location. It reduced the risk if any one location was discovered."

"Could they . . ." Thia's voice faltered, and she didn't specify who 'they' were, but she didn't have to. "Could they have somehow gotten here before us?"

"We should leave," Molly said, and she reached out and took Jake's hand as she took a quick step back down the stairs and back toward the exit.

"But we have nowhere else to go!" Thia moaned softly.

Suddenly, there was no more time for conversation or debate. The safe room door flew open, and a figure stepped out of the light.

EVIE

Evie knew she had to stop crying.

"I've got to get a hold of myself," she whispered, clutching at her stomach. "This isn't doing anyone any good." Tears dripped down her nose. She had already read Bea's e-mail a hundred times, but she leaned in close to her laptop and read it again.

She should have known. There had been clues, she realized, looking back over their last conversation. She should have guessed what Bea was planning. She should have stopped her before it was too late.

Too late. The words echoed in her mind over and over. She had pressed reply, started writing Bea back, sentence after disjointed sentence a hundred times, asking her to reconsider, begging her to come back. But it was too late. Bea would never read her e-mail. Wouldn't respond to her texts.

The one person Evie had left in all the world was gone.

Loneliness and loss cut like carving knives at her insides, emptying her out, leaving her feeling hollow and forsaken. She had never felt so alone.

Maybe I could have helped if she had told me, Evie thought, wiping her eyes with her sleeve. *What if there was something that I could have done? And now I can't even tell her goodbye.*

Evie felt the misery like a churning black tar, swirling in her chest. It burned, choking out the air inside her. She didn't know how to live with loss like this, and she didn't want to learn.

Then, through the regret and the tears and the heart-wrenching sorrow, Evie heard a noise right outside the door.

In an instant, she was on her feet. Every muscle quivered, and her ears strained, but she couldn't quite believe her own senses. She hadn't really heard anything. She was just upset—hysterical, even. She was imagining things.

Then the noise came again.

Footsteps creeping up the secret staircase. Shuffling steps, shattering the silence.

Intruders breaching the one, minuscule corner of the universe she had managed to make her own.

Evie straightened up. She couldn't take this anymore. Fear and grief coalesced like twisting snakes inside her, fusing and transforming into an anger that burned.

"Really, Universe?" she hissed under her breath. "You *really* aren't done fucking with me yet?"

She walked over to the door and stared at it.

No one should have known where the safe room was located. She didn't want to believe it was possible. But her ears told her that someone was already on the stairs. This room was fortified; the locks were built to withstand almost any assault. But blockading yourself in a locked safe room only works if help was coming. It was made so you could hunker down, hold out just long enough for the Calvary to come to the rescue.

But Evie was alone.

Andrew had never meant for her to have access to the Echoes safe rooms. She had stolen the key to get in. No one was coming to save her from the menace creeping up the stairs.

She had her own plans in place . . . for if the worst happened.

But she had to *know*.

She stood behind the door and braced her legs. She would open it just long enough to see. Then she would do whatever needed to be done.

As quietly as she could, she unlocked the door. Then she took a deep breath and flung it open.

She wasn't sure what she had been expecting, but it wasn't the four dirty, beleaguered figures she found on the stairs.

"Who are you?" she cried, but then her eyes adjusted to the dark and she recognized two of the faces: Thia, the woman who ran the tavern at the Refuge, and Molly, the woman from the bar. "What happened?" Evie gasped, and stepped back, opening the door wider to let them in.

They rushed inside, and Evie slammed the door shut and threw the locks back into place. When she turned to face them, the expressions on their faces told her half the story before Thia even spoke. Molly and the man she was with fell heavily into chairs at the table, their faces so white that Evie wondered if they might pass out.

"Steele found the Refuge," Thia said, her voice dull with shock. She twisted her fingers together so tightly that Evie could see her knuckles turn white. "He and the other Legacies attacked. We got out," she swallowed hard. "Just barely. I don't know what happened to anybody else."

"Andrew?" Evie asked, surprised to feel her throat go tight. She had been so, so angry at Andrew. He had been a stupid, pig-headed idiot, and he had thrown her out onto the street. She shouldn't care about him. Not anymore. But he had saved her life not so long ago, and Evie's heart constricted with fear for him, no matter what her mind was saying.

Thia just shrugged helplessly. "I don't know."

"You got out," Evie repeated slowly, her mind moving sluggishly, not wanting to process what this meant. "But if the Legacies found the Refuge, then they'll track you. They'll come here."

It was all too much, and in a dazed sort of horror, she walked over to the attic's one window and gazed out. It was dark out, still the middle of the night. The moon was shining, though, and outside on the campus grounds there were lights on in front of the library and spaced periodically along the sidewalks. It was three in the morning, and the campus was quiet. No one moved outside. Evie could hear water splashing in the fountain out front. Everything looked peaceful, but Evie knew that meant nothing.

"No one followed us." A man she remembered vaguely . . . Matt . . . said. He pulled a chair away from the table and fell into it. "We got out through the tunnels, just like we practiced. We followed the evacuation plan. We're safe."

Evie couldn't help it; she laughed. "You have no idea what you're talking about," she told him bitterly. "You aren't *safe*. None of us are *safe*." She gestured around the room, her gesture including Thia and Molly and her companion. "The Refuge has fallen. If Andrew isn't dead already, then by now he really wishes that he was. And even if you weren't followed, if the Legacies found the Refuge, then they can find the safe rooms, too."

"Listen," Matt told her, holding out his hands. "I know you're scared. You have every right to be. I won't lie to you: I'm terrified, too. But I trust Andrew. He knew this day might come, and he planned for it. He's saved my ass before, and his evacuation plan got us out alive tonight. They got us this far. We need to call and check in. Find out who else got out."

"How can you be sure that's safe to do?" Molly protested.

"The number is to a secure location, and we have code words set up to use when we call in. It's as near to fool-proof as any plan can be. And we can't just stay holed up here forever." He slid his phone out of his pocket. "But my phone isn't working."

"The safe room walls are reinforced," Evie told him. "You won't be able to get any reception in here."

"Then I'll have to go back out," Matt said, standing up. Evie could tell from his expression he wasn't very happy about going back out into the dark. "Just long enough to call."

"But we just got here," Thia cried. "I thought the whole point of a safe room was to stay inside it!"

"If Evie's right that the Legacies can find the safe rooms, then we might not be safe here anyway," Matt answered grimly. "If we don't call in, then we can't know."

"I'll go with you," Molly's companion said, and Molly whipped around to face him. "I can keep a look out for you while you're on the phone."

"It's too dangerous, Jake," Molly protested. He shrugged.

"It's safer than just bolting out of here into the dark. Or hunkering down, and hoping really hard that everything turns out okay." He touched her cheek lightly. "I'm just going to watch Matt's back. I'll be alright."

Molly bit her lip, then nodded.

Jake gestured toward the window. "Where are we, anyway?"

"The University of Maryland," Evie answered him. "McKeldon Library," she felt herself blushing. "I knew there was a safe room up here and I . . . I stole one of the keys before Andrew kicked me out. Just in case I ended up needing it." She gestured to the corner of the attic, where a sleeping bag had been spread out on the floor, next to a small pile of clothes and personal belongings. "Which I did. Obviously."

As she spoke, Jake's face paled. He looked like he'd been punched in the stomach.

"What's wrong?" Molly asked him. He shook his head.

"Nothing," he answered, his voice gruff. "It's just that I was a student here, a while ago." He gave a pained, bitter smile. "It didn't work out so great for me."

"If we're going to do this," Matt said, stepping toward the door, "we should go now."

Jake nodded, shoved his hands deep in his pockets, and hunched his shoulders as he followed behind Matt.

"We'll be back real soon," he promised as Molly watched them unlock the door and step out onto the staircase with distinct unease.

As soon as the door shut behind them, Evie turned and looked around the room, forcing herself to be cold. Calculating. Andrew had planned for the worst-case scenario.

Evie had some plans of her own.

Being busy helped her heart rate slow. Moving with determined speed, Evie began walking the aisles of the shelved books. She pulled out one volume, and then another. She created a pile in the center of the long wooden table. She had to be careful about her notes—those were the most dangerous of all. She yanked notebooks from her bag, gathered others from the shelves in a large armful, and carried them to the table. But she had left other notes scattered around the room, or tucked into books to mark the page. She searched, methodically piling sheet after scribbled-on sheet of paper she found down on top of the table.

"What are you doing?" Molly asked, after watching her uncertainly for a minute. Thia had put her head down on her arms on the tabletop and seemed to be asleep.

Evie knew better than to answer directly. "You don't know Steele," she said instead. "I do. There is nothing worse than being in his power. Nothing." She shuddered with certainty and slapped another sheet of paper down.

"What do you mean, you know him?" Molly asked, her eyes following Evie's frantic movements closely.

"My father is the head of one of the most powerful Legacy houses in the country," Evie explained, not looking up. She didn't want to know what emotions were flashing across Molly's face. "I was supposed to be his heir." Evie closed her eyes and let the memories come. "I was happy for a long time. In some ways, that's the worst part of it. I always felt treasured. Loved. My dad was a kind of distant, benevolent figure. My mom was always fussing over me. I thought it would always be that way. I didn't realize they would only love me as long as I was good for something."

"But I got older, and the powers I was supposed to have never materialized. Gradually, things changed. My mother's anxiety turned to panic. My father's eyes turned to ice."

Evie looked down at the tabletop, covered with all the frenzied notes she had taken. Now, all her big plans and great ambitions just seemed like some poor, delusional girl's fever-dream.

"That's when they took me to Steele."

"Wait," Molly said, her eyebrows climbing. "Your parents *took* you to him?"

"For *treatment*," Evie let sarcasm fill her voice like venom. "He's a scientist, didn't you know? A genius. He was my parents' last hope, the last chance to change me from a useless cripple into the heir they always wanted. Steele told them that I might have latent abilities; that certain . . . experiences might force those abilities to surface." Evie laughed, mostly to hide the sob that had somehow inched up into her throat. "He called it therapy. I begged . . ." her voice broke, and she had to swallow hard before she could keep going. "I begged them not to. I had been a very sheltered child. I wasn't used to pain. But even then, there was a part of me that thought it would be worth it if it meant I could have their love back again. If it meant I could keep being their daughter."

Evie turned away, pretending to lean close to examine the books on the shelf behind her. But really, her eyes were too clouded with tears for her to see anything. "Nothing worked," she went on. "After a while, Steele ran some tests. When the results came back, he told them I wasn't salvageable. But that my genes were good. He suggested that they 'breed' me." Evie screwed her eyes shut, trying not to remember the way the room had seemed to spin around her while she spoke or the way her mother had refused to meet her eyes.

"They took me home and locked me in my room. A few nights later, a man came in. I knew him a little, enough to be afraid. The funny thing is, my father had always hated Troy; had always said that Troy was cruel and stupid. A mindless tough guy. But, I guess he made the highest bid. Anyway, suddenly there he was, standing over my bed. Leering down at me."

"He didn't rape me. He said he hadn't paid for that part. Yet. But that he was entitled to sample the goods before the deal was sealed. And he . . . touched me." Evie felt nauseous and her head swam. She leaned her forehead against the cool wood of the bookcase. She breathed in the scent of paper and old books, taking what comfort she could.

"I screamed. I fought. I called for my parents . . . but no one came. They must have heard— they were right down the hall. But they didn't come."

Evie hadn't felt Molly coming up behind her, but now Molly's arm wrapped around her shoulders in a tight embrace. Evie leaned into her, surprised by how natural it felt to take comfort from her. She didn't know Molly that well. But, somehow, she knew that Molly understood.

"How did you get away?" Molly asked quietly, after a minute.

Evie smiled and wiped her eyes. "Andrew," she said. "Of course, Andrew. I don't know how he knew or even why he cared. Andrew has always been passionate about saving the Echoes, and I was never one of them. But somehow, for some reason, he still came for me."

She laughed now, a watery, weak laugh of disbelief. "He came to my window in the middle of the night. I didn't even know who he was, but I would have followed just about anyone at that point. His car was parked in the street with the engine running. I'm still not sure why he saved me." Evie shrugged. "Maybe he knew I could help him with his research. Whatever his reason was, I'll never be able to stop being grateful to him for getting me out that night. No matter what other mistakes he might make."

Evie shivered as she realized by now Andrew might very well

be dead. In that instant, she felt her anger at him dwindle to nothing.

"Is that what all of this is?" Molly asked, turning to look around the attic with wide eyes. "Your research, trying to find the goblet that Andrew's so obsessed with?"

Evie shook herself and forced her body back into motion. Drowning in her memories now would not help anything. She pulled two more books off the shelf and stacked them carefully in the center of the table. She stood back and ran her eyes over the volumes and piles of paper she had collected. She wanted to be sure she hadn't missed anything. She leaned down and let her fingers brush against the canister she kept under the table. It made her feel safer, knowing it was there.

"Not really," she answered Molly absentmindedly, as she mentally ran down a checklist of the most important books. "Andrew was trying to figure out the goblet's location. But I figured that out months and months ago."

"What?" Molly cried, and the surprise in her voice jerked Evie out of her reprieve. "That isn't what Andrew told me. He said you only found more dead-ends."

"Andrew never *listens*," Evie said with a frustrated shake of her head. She reached up and pulled the USB key that she wore around her neck out from under her shirt, and held it up for Molly to see. "The location of the goblet wasn't even that hard to discover. I just had to put the pieces together. I've had all that information on here for months. But Andrew never understood what I was trying to tell him." She tucked the USB key back under her shirt with a sigh. "We shouldn't be searching for the goblet at all. We should be searching for them." And she pointed to an open book on the table showing a black and white drawing of a figure with black wings spread wide and long clawed fingers reaching out toward the reader.

"You want to find the Watchers?" Molly asked, her words slow and uncertain. "Why would you try to find monsters?"

"What if they aren't monsters at all?" Evie asked, and despite everything, she felt excitement rise inside her. "What if the legends are wrong? What if the things the Legacies have told us about them are lies? Think about it this way, Molly," she tapped her finger against the page, "the Legacies want power more than anything else. They always have. And the Watchers have always held them back from using their power. What if the resentment that the Legacies feel about that has twisted the stories we've been told? Poisoned them? So that we've always believed something that isn't true at all?"

"But if that's true," Molly said, her eyes flicking over Evie's notes with new interest, "why don't the Watchers intercede? The Legacies are killing people. Doing horrible things. If the Watchers object, why don't they do something to stop it?"

"I don't know," Evie admitted. "But there's only one way to find out."

"So your plan is what, exactly?" Molly asked. "To figure out the super-secret hiding place of these beings that can take away your will forever. And then just walk up to them and ask them some questions? You have to know how crazy that sounds, right?"

Evie walked over to the window and stood, gazing up into the night. Clouds had blown across the sky and covered the moon, obscuring it. The wind had picked up. The branches of the trees on the campus mall whipped from side to side. Evie thought she could hear a distant rumble of thunder.

"I'm not sure," she answered honestly. "I don't know if I ever had a plan for exactly what I would do once I found them. Mostly I just had this hope: that there was someone out there who could help. That there was a force just as powerful as the monsters chasing me." She lay her hand against the glass. She could feel the cold seeping through the window pane, and the pressure of wind building on the other side the glass. Evie shook her head. "Anyway, my plans don't matter anymore. The Refuge has fallen. And a storm is coming."

BEA

It turned out that dying was harder than she had imagined. In her imagination, she had seen herself sailing away. She had pictured the perfect arc of her dive as she cast herself into the water, the serenity on her face as she pulled the water up and around her, like a great blue blanket that wrapped around her and pulled her gently toward eternal sleep.

The problem, she admitted to herself on the third day of her journey, was that she did not actually *want* to die.

She sure as hell did not want to sicken slowly, to be pumped full of chemicals or punctured with tubes, to watch the silent horror on her parents' faces as she choked and hacked and inched her way to death. A quick, clean death, one of her own choosing, had seemed immeasurably better than that in her cool, calm reasoning. There had been freedom in the feeling of abandon, of defiance. But standing on the deck in the cool, pale blue mists of early morning, she had realized the truth.

She wanted more. More of the smooth, cool water shimmering around her. More of the sun warming the deck under her toes. She wanted the wind as it brushed against the naked skin on her head and the puckered scars on her chest. The damp spray that kissed her, the fresh smell of the sea . . . it was sweet. Too sweet to turn away from.

And hope, which she thought she had squashed so resolutely, found its way into her heart again. She felt it pulling her through the early morning mist, felt it tugging at the corners of her mind, no matter how much she tried to ignore it. What could she possibly hope for? Her grandfather's ghost seemed to stand defeated beside her, hands buried deep in his pockets, shaking his head. She didn't know what, but she knew that she was looking for it. For some call that beckoned a part of her deep inside, that had no words, but pulled and pulled.

She didn't even know where she was anymore. She hadn't planned to journey so far. She meant to go just far enough away to have solitude and quiet when she took her plunge. Whenever she saw land, she sailed away from it. When she saw another ship, she sped up and went the other way. She felt suspended between two worlds. She no longer belonged to the land of the living. But she didn't want to leave it.

So she kept sailing, peering into the distance, trying to find some way to drop anchor and keep her hold of the peace she discovered in this strange state of limbo.

The storm built up slowly. It was a sign, and Bea knew it. The clouds gathered, black and gray above her, and Bea felt as though the storm was a friend reaching, slipping her keys out of her hand, and gently pulling her from the party.

Time to go, now, the wind whispered as it whipped around her. *You've had enough.*

No, she answered, and tied down the sails.

She thought that she would never run again. Now the wind streamed against her face as she sailed before the storm. There was a joy in it, a savage freedom. But no matter what she did, or how hard she tried to steer the boat toward clearer weather, the gray clouds slowly turned to black above her. Soon the rain was pounding against the wood, and the wind shoved the boat from side to side. Bea was busy every minute, slipping on bare feet as she ran back and forth across the deck. The storm was too big, and soon she knew there was no way she could escape it. Maybe her grandfather would have known how to sail safely through it, but his ghost could only stand by helplessly and watch.

Crammed away in some distant part of her, she felt her fear pulsing, but ignored it. She had too much to do.

The clouds lit up with brilliant lightning, and then the sky went black. Blind in the darkness, Bea couldn't scramble around anymore. She grabbed tight to the railing and pressed herself against it, fighting the wind that tried, again and again, to toss her over the side. It seemed she huddled there forever, head down, occasionally glancing up at the sky looking for . . . something. The moon would sometimes peek down at her, its light pale yellow and disapproving.

When the cracking sound came, Bea was surprised and, despite herself, horrified. She had not thought of this. She had only imagined herself being thrown from the deck, disappearing into the water. It never occurred to her that the boat would be destroyed. The boat was her friend, her companion; she had imagined it drifting on peacefully without her. Now she felt the wood moaning beneath her feet, and mourned for it more than for herself, as rocks she had never seen smashed into them, and she was thrown into the black, choking water.

Some part of her seemed to wrench out of her head and float above the water, disinterested, observing, as the impact of the water forced the air from her lungs.

She sucked in salt.

It stung her throat; burned her. She coughed and gasped beneath the water, waving her arms and pushing against the swirling waves that held her down.

She did not want this . . . any of it. She wanted life, long and happy and full of light.

I haven't had enough, she thought desperately, her mind confused and wandering. *I need more.*

She only fought her way back to the surface once. Fighting for air, clawing at the night sky, beyond reason and hope, desperate for one more breath, for a little air to soothe her lungs.

The sky was black wind; the water was thick with debris. Splintered wood slammed into her, cutting her cheek. A cloud moved, and for a second she could see the moon.

She looked up, her mind dazed with pain and confusion. For a second, she thought she saw a menacing form, outlined against the sky, its black wings spread wide.

Then the water closed over her head, and the current pulled her down. Bea fought, screaming her defiance into the watery silence.

But in the end, all she could do was close her eyes.

EVIE

"Something isn't right," Jake announced, hurrying back into the room with Matt right behind him.

"What?" Molly spun to face him. "What's wrong?"

At the table, Thia opened her eyes and looked around blearily.

"Matt got through to Tyler, just for a minute," Jake said. "He just asked who we had with us, and then told us to stay put. He said that everything is still chaos and they're still trying to figure out who made it out. And now look." He pointed over Evie's shoulder, toward the small round window at the far end of the attic.

Evie made it there first.

"It's the lights," Evie said. "All the streetlights outside have gone out."

The darkness had thickened so much that campus mall might as well have disappeared. Impenetrable black surrounded everything.

For a moment, no one spoke. They just stood and stared at the blackness. Evie strained to hear the sound of feet, or of cars driving past. Even the sound of the water falling in the fountain outside. But she couldn't hear anything at all, except for the quiet, strained breathing of the people around her, and her own panicked heartbeat, pulsing in her ears.

"It's Steele," Evie said, though the feeling of tension, rising in the room like the pressure of a building storm, told her they already knew. "He's found us."

"Oh my God," Thia jumped to her feet. "But . . . the door downstairs is fortified and locked. Right?" She looked from one face to another, searching for reassurance. "He can't just walk in. We'll be safe for now at least. Right?"

Then the night's perfect silence was shattered by the low, drawn out click of a key sliding into a lock. Moving like one person, everyone but Evie turned to stare in the direction of the stairs, identical expressions of shock and horror on their faces.

But Evie didn't turn to look.

For months, she had lain awake at night, bathed in the moonlight that streamed in through the little attic window, playing out one worst-case scenario after another in her mind. She had lived through the terror of this moment so many times already. Now that it had really come, there was something familiar in the horror that crept along her skin. It was almost a relief.

She had been running from this situation for so long. But Steele was here. The worst had happened. Now all she had to do was face it.

For all she knew, Steele had brought Troy along. He could be hurrying up the stairs toward her right now, eager to claim her and break her will forever. But Evie wouldn't let that happen. Whatever else it cost her, she would keep her mind and body as her own.

She knew what she had to do. She reached under the table, pulled out the first canister, and got to work.

"Evie?" Molly asked, her voice full of confusion and concern. But Evie didn't look up. Carefully, she unscrewed the cap. The smell was so strong her eyes immediately began to water. She worked carefully, making sure the liquid spread evenly over all the books and papers she had gathered. She couldn't afford to make any mistakes.

"Holy shit. What are you doing?" Evie heard Matt cry out. But she didn't look up. She had to be sure the gasoline soaked into everything evenly. It splashed onto her shoes, onto her clothes and fingers, but she didn't care.

"Evie?" Molly asked, her voice filled more with worry than fear. Evie looked up. Molly had stepped closer to her; her hand half stretched out in Evie's direction. Thia was backing toward the door, a look of horror on her face.

"I'm burning it," she told them. "All of it. My notes, research. The books. Everything. Steele can't ever get access to any of this. If he's here, that means it's time." The first canister was empty. Evie tossed it aside and pulled the second canister out from under the table.

"Wait a second," Matt cried. "You can't just set all that stuff on fire. You'll kill us all!"

"You don't understand," Evie stopped just long enough to look up at him. "Steele's a monster. He can kill with a word. And this . . ." she pointed at the gasoline-soaked papers. "This would make him even more powerful than he is already. I can't let that happen. I'm the one who uncovered these secrets. This is my responsibility." She swallowed hard and began to pour more gasoline out onto the table. "There's a door, on the landing of the fourth floor. They're coming now, but if you can get there before they do, you can use your key to get out. The door opens into the main library stacks. You can get out the main library doors if you hurry."

"Okay, then we've got to go now." Matt said. "Maybe we can make it back to the tunnels." He slid the door open as quietly as he could. Thia and Jake stood next to him at the doorway.

Molly turned back to Evie and held out her hand. "Come with us," she urged. "You don't have to stay here."

Emotion surged in Evie's chest, and for a second she almost

considered it. But she had planned for this, and she knew just what she had to do.

"I can't," she said, wishing that her voice wasn't shaking. "I've got a different plan."

"To do what? Set yourself on fire?" Molly demanded, her eyes flashing. "I know you've been through a lot. Maybe right now you feel like this is your only way out. But you're wrong. It doesn't have to be that way. Come with us. Please."

"You don't understand. It's different for me."

Jake was practically vibrating with impatience. "We've got to go right now Molly," he urged her. "I can hear them coming up the stairs." But Molly's eyes were still fastened on Evie.

"Why?" she demanded. "Why can't you come with us right now?"

"All the information that's in these papers, these books," Evie gestured to the gasoline-soaked stacks on the table top. "All that information is inside *me,* too." She lay a hand against her chest. "I know all of it . . . I remember everything. Every word, every secret. I couldn't forget it, even if I wanted to. If Steele got control of me now, he could force me to tell him everything. I would be handing him the key to power like nothing he's ever imagined. I can't let that happen. I can't take that risk." She blinked hard, refusing to let tears rise in her eyes. "I know you understand."

"No," Molly said, stubbornly, shaking her head. "I don't understand. You're wrong, and you don't have to do this. You're a fighter." Molly swallowed hard. "Like me. Don't give up now."

The last canister was empty, and the fumes were making her head swim. Evie pulled a book of matches from her pocket. With a sure, quick motion, she struck the match. She held it in front of her and smiled at Molly over the flame.

"Oh, don't worry," she told her. "I am fighting."

There was a clatter of feet coming closer on the stairs.

"Come on!" Jake cried, yanking on Molly so hard he was practically dragging her from the room. "We've got to go!" Thia and

Matt were backing away quickly, already half hidden by the shadows in the hall.

"Go," Evie told her. And she let the match fall from her fingers.

Molly gave a strangled cry of frustration and took a stumbling step back. Jake pulled her away. A second later they disappeared down the stairs.

Evie backed toward the door slowly, waiting to be sure the flames caught and built. The heat mounted quickly, pushing against her as the fire grew fast and greedy, spreading it's red, grasping fingers across the room. She coughed and stepped back, shielding her eyes from the sting of the smoke. The blaze crackled and swelled. Evie heard the glass of the round attic window shatter as heat pressed against it.

She knew she didn't have long but, still, she gave herself one last second to gaze around the room that had fast become her home. All her things were here; every single possession she had left. A few pictures she had taken with her the night Andrew had helped her run away. Her sleeping bag, and the notes and books that had almost felt like friends. This room had been her haven. At night, the moonlight would stream through the round window, and she would sleep, surrounded by its light. She looked at her little nook regretfully, bidding it goodbye. She had loved it here; the smell of the books, the quiet feeling of lying in her sleeping bag and gazing at the moon. But the fire was spreading quickly.

This room would never shelter her again.

Evie spun on her heel and darted up the stairs.

She could hear yelling, and the sound of feet pounding on the stairs was dangerously close now. She sprinted, wheezing from the smoke and the strain of running, but despite the adrenaline and the fear and the smoke-filled stairway, Evie's mind was perfectly clear.

She knew she was going to die.

It felt inevitable. Fated. As though everything she had ever been through in her entire life had always been leading her straight into this moment.

Somehow, that didn't make it any easier to bear.

She reached the top of the stairs, threw the door open and raced out onto the roof.

Twelve stories up. The sky was black and cloudless. The moon loomed above, and the cold air bit at her skin. Her feet slowed as she approached the ledge.

Evie grabbed hold and hoisted herself up onto it, scraping her palms on the rough gray stone. The ledge had seemed wide when her feet had been safely planted on the roof, but standing on the edge with the darkness billowing out in front of her like a great black cape, Evie felt the world stagger and tip.

I have to jump now, she told herself. *Before Steele can catch up to me. Before he can so much as speak a word.*

She inched a little further out, trying to find the will to take that last step out into the darkness. She knew just what her life would be if she did not take this final escape. But . . . still. The darkness before her seemed like the black, angry face of some greedy god, waiting to reach up and snap her in its jaws, consume her and leave her body in bloody, shattered fragments on the pavement far below.

Her feet refused to move.

Evie thought of her mother. She remembered sitting on the couch while her mother braided her hair. Longing, sharper than any knife, rose inside her. Longing for the one who had given birth to her, kissed her hurts when she was small, who had rocked her and promised everything would be alright. The kisses, the love—none of it had been enough. Her mother's love had been conditional. When Evie's gift didn't materialize, her mother's love had dried up and fallen away.

Gasping for breath, trying desperately to find the courage she needed now, she lay a hand against her chest. Her fingers touched something hard and cold.

Evie looked down, her head reeling. All her planning. All the steps she had taken to make sure that every bit of her research was burned, that every clue that could have led Steele to power was destroyed.

But she had forgotten the USB key that still hung around her neck.

Evie pulled it off, and stared at it, horrified, just as the door clattered open behind her.

Instinctively, Evie opened her hand. The USB key fell from her fingers and plummeted into the darkness. *Let it shatter on the pavement,* she prayed. *Let it be destroyed.*

Then she turned to face him.

Steele's chest was heaving as his eyes swept the rooftop. They missed nothing, running over her, coldness and calculation in his gaze.

"Find the others," he called back over his shoulder. "The situation here is under control."

He closed the door behind him calmly and leaned back against it, folding his arms over his chest. Studying her.

"Stay away from me," Evie warned him.

Smiling as though she had said something funny, Steele took a slow step forward.

"No!" Evie backed up until her heels hung over the edge. "I made this choice long ago, Steele. I'll die first. My parents should have told you that before they sent you after me."

Steele's lips pulled back from his teeth in a wide smirk. The darkness cast strange shadows on his face, and his eyes glinted weirdly in the moonlight. Evie could hear the fire raging in the library, crackling beneath their feet.

"Your parents did not 'send' me," Steele growled. "I am not their lap dog. If I wanted you dead, Evie, you would be dead already. You know that. You know how easy it would be." He smiled. "But I'd rather have you on your knees." He inched a little closer. "I brokered a deal," Steele tsked at her, as though she were a disobedient child. "I negotiated your sale to Troy. Your subsequent disappearance was an embarrassment to me. I even had to return my percentage of your price. At first, that was the only reason that I hunted you. But now, I've heard you have even more to offer me than just the lottery ticket that's buried in your genes. From what I've been told, you've become quite the little scholar, Evie. There are so many things that you can tell me, once I've taught you your true place in this world." Steele smiled broadly, showing all his teeth. "I can hardly wait. And of course, Troy can still have you. Once I've had my turn. Now, enough of this charade." He beckoned to her imperiously. "We both know that you aren't going to jump. I remember enough from your therapy sessions to be sure of that."

"Go to hell," Evie spat. "You don't know me."

"Always trembling," Steele went on, as though she hadn't spoken. "Always crying and begging me to stop. There's no fight in you. No strength." His face darkened, and his eyes flashed. "Now you're wasting my time. And that's starting to make me angry."

"What do you know about strength?" Evie cried, her fear and anger coalescing into fury. "You're a monster. What will you ever be, except a killer and a demon? What have you ever done but use your power to hurt and to destroy? I *am* strong, Steele. Stronger than you will ever be, and in ways you could never hope to understand. Strong enough to get away from you!"

She turned and opened her arms wide, inviting the darkness into her, as though it could numb the pain she knew would come.

She sobbed once. And then Evie hurled herself over the edge.

She screamed as she fell, clutching at air that slid through her fingers. The ground rushed up to meet her, the rest of the world a shapeless gray blur that streamed past the edges of her sight.

"Please, please, please . . ." she screamed in her mind, though her mouth could form no words, and she didn't even know what she was praying for.

Something slammed into her from behind, something hard as rock and hot as fire, knocking all the breath from her body.

An arm wrapped around her waist, and with a sudden jerk upwards, Evie was no longer falling . . . she was being lifted through the air. Stars blurred into streams of light as she soared higher. With a gasp, she wrenched her head around to stare behind her.

"Roman?" Evie cried.

Black leather wings stretched out from his back. He had shed his shirt and the jacket which, Evie realized, he must have worn to hide his wings. His face was different from what she remembered, his eyes were wider, his eyebrows thicker. Where his hand pressed against her belly, Evie could feel long, curved claws stretching out against her skin.

He met her eyes, and flinched, as though it hurt to have her see him. Evie stared back at him, slack-jawed and dazed, until a moment later, when he landed on a nearby rooftop and gently set her down.

As soon as her feet touched the solid surface, Evie was scrambling to put distance between them.

"You don't have to be afraid," Roman signed, his wings perfectly still behind him. *"I don't want to hurt you."*

For a long moment, Evie could only stare. The adrenaline still coursing through her body seemed to make her brain move at a break-neck pace. She lifted her hands to sign back to him, then lowered them, slowly, as several things clicked into place.

"You're a Siren," Evie gasped, clutching her chest with her hands as she tried to get air into lungs that felt too tight to breathe. She didn't need to sign to him; she realized that now. "You've been watching me, haven't you?" she gasped. "Using sign, pretending you were deaf so you could be around humans."

Roman flinched. *"None of that matters now,"* he told her. *"You have a chance to be safe now. From Steele, from . . . everyone. You can run. Steele didn't see me save you. He thinks you're dead. And I won't tell my people anything about you. You can get away, and start over."*

Evie stared at him, her mind spinning. She turned her head to look out over the buildings. They were so high up. It had felt like they had only been in the air for a moment, but the university was a speck in the distance. Roman must have flown with incredible speed. She thought she could just make out orange flames darting from the library windows.

"You're not supposed to be doing this, are you?" she asked, the words a little halting as she struggled to process everything. "You're breaking your own rules right now, by talking to me. By saving me."

Roman's fingers clenched into fists. He didn't answer.

"I tried to learn as much about Siren law as I could," Evie went on. "I couldn't find much. But I know that you can't just reveal yourself like this." She craned her head to the side, trying to see his face more clearly through the shadows. "What are you risking by doing this for me?" she asked. "What would happen to you if the other Sirens found out?"

Roman's wings stretched out, flapping once behind him and creating a sudden breeze that pushed the curls away from Evie's face. *"I serve my king and my people,"* he signed, lifting his chin. *"But my life is my own, to risk as I will."* He looked away, as though he couldn't bear to meet her eyes. *"I didn't come to this place to destroy innocents."*

Warmth sparked deep in Evie's chest. It had been so long since she felt that once familiar feeling, she had to stop and think for a moment before she could name it.

Hope.

"I was right," Evie whispered. She took another step closer to Roman; she almost wasn't afraid of him now. "You aren't monsters."

Roman's lips twisted into a sad smile.

"We try very hard not to be," he admitted.

Evie took a deep breath. She was about to do something very, very stupid. But she had risked so much already, and the small spark of hope in her chest was building into a steady blaze.

"Thank you for the risk you are willing to take for me, Roman," she said, opening her eyes and throwing back her shoulders. "But no."

"What do you mean, Evie?" Roman asked, his eyes wide with worry. *"Don't throw your life away!"*

"You have a king, right?" Evie asked eagerly, and Roman nodded, his eyes wary, confusion plain on his face. "I want to talk to him." Evie explained. "There are things he needs to know."

"You don't understand," Roman signed furiously. *"What you're asking me to do is totally forbidden. Bringing you into our city would go against all of our laws!"*

"Aren't you breaking those laws already?" Evie asked. Summoning all of her courage, she edged closer to him. He held perfectly still, as if afraid the slightest movement would scare her away. His face didn't seem as different as she had thought when she was standing closer. Slowly she reached out and touched his shoulder. She hadn't been imagining it—his skin was hot to the touch.

Roman reached up, caught her fingers, and gently moved her hand away.

"What you're asking me to do now is different," he explained. *"I can choose to take my own risks. But you are asking me to put you in danger."*

"Shouldn't that be my choice?" Evie asked, folding her hands in front of her. "I know the chance I'm taking. It's worth it to me. I'm asking you to help me, Roman. Please."

Roman looked at her for several long, silent moments. Evie didn't look away.

"You're sure this is what you want?" he asked her.

"Yes," Evie breathed. "This is what I've been searching for. I'm sure."

Roman ran a hand through his hair, shaking his head as something akin to laughter lit his eyes. *"This is the craziest thing I've ever heard . . . a human who actually wants to enter our city."*

Evie said nothing, just waited patiently while he thought.

"But if it is what you want . . ." he stepped forward and put a gentle hand on her hip. *"Then we will take this risk together."*

He raised his eyebrows in silent invitation, and Evie wrapped her arms around his neck. She could feel her cheeks burning as the heat of his body pressed through her shirt, and his arms pulled her tighter against him. Roman's chest vibrated as his wings beat faster.

The wind whipped against Evie's face and hair and she gasped, looking with wonder at a moon that suddenly did not seem so far away. And though they were flying fast toward a future that Evie could barely imagine, she felt that spark of hope burn, brighter than ever, in her chest.

MOLLY

Molly hadn't known she was afraid of fire.

Leaving Evie behind tore at her heart. But she respected Evie's choice and, deep down, she understood it. And so, when there was nothing else that she could do, she turned away, clutched Jake's hand tightly in her own, and followed Matt and Thia down the stairs. Fear made their feet swift. They found the door that Evie told them about quickly. Matt slid his key into the lock, threw the door open, and darted through. Thia and Jake pushed the door shut behind them, and Matt locked it again. Then the four stood, shoulder to shoulder, standing with their ears pressed against the door, breathing hard, and listening. Sure enough, mere seconds later they heard the scuffle and the scrape of heavy boots rushing past them on the other side of the stairs, up and up, toward the attic.

Molly could hear the crackle of flames in the silence.

When the noise had passed them, Molly reached out and took Jake's hand in hers.

"Alright," she whispered, squeezing his fingers tight and nodding to Matt and Thia. "Now we run."

They pelted through the dim library, passing towering shelves packed tight with countless volumes. Strange shadows lingered in the corners and seemed to wave and shimmer as they passed. The faster they ran, the more Molly felt something unclench in her chest. The movement felt good, and she welcomed the burn in her legs, the catch in her lungs. This was familiar; running was something she knew how to do. She was good at it, and as they ran she believed, right down to the core of her being, that she and Jake would be okay.

Then the smoke came.

One moment they were nearing the wide staircase at the center of the building. *Only seven floors down, and then free.* Molly told herself.

Then she squinted. Was she imagining it, or was it even dimmer than it had been a moment before? Suddenly, Jake coughed, the sound deep and wrenching. Molly stopped short, staring around them. In the semi-darkness, she hadn't even noticed the ominous gray haze that had formed above them, and now swirled and darkened like a sudden storm.

"Keep low!" she called to Jake, hunching over to try to keep her face in the fresher air as they started to run again. The smell of burning paper and wood thickened around them. Molly's eyes stung and watered, and she wiped her face with the back of her hand, trying to keep the pace of their flight even though her chest throbbed.

She looked around a second later, and the smoke was so thick around them that she couldn't see Matt and Thia anymore.

"Where are they?" Jake coughed.

Fire alarms screamed, blaring out a frantic, pulsating warning that echoed against the library walls. Red lights flashed from the walls, and overhead an emergency sprinkler system activated. A steady stream of water assailed them from above.

"We just have to keep going!" Molly said, raising her voice so he could hear her over the din. "We can still make it."

"Okay," Jake called back, "two more flights to go."

Molly pushed sodden hair out of her eyes and held Jake's hand tighter in her own. They ran together, their feet slipping on the wet, marble stairs, coughing and gasping for breath in the smoke-filled air.

Then Molly heard a strange sound coming from above them. A roaring, groaning sound that reminded her of thunder.

She looked up.

A fissure opened in the ceiling above them, and brilliant orange light seared through the darkness. For a single heartbeat, Molly froze, staring up at the fracture that bled fire and smoke. Then the ceiling crumbled.

Huge chunks of cement fell onto the stairs in front of them, blocking their way, shaking the staircase like an earthquake.

"HOLY FUCK!" Jake yelled, yanking her back as he scrambled backwards. Molly cried out in wordless horror, tripping over her own feet and nearly falling as she tried to escape the flames.

"We've got to find another way out!" she screamed.

Flame streamed out of the hole in the ceiling, like a hungry dragon crouching low and snapping hungry jaws. It seemed to sense the nearness of more kindling and arced toward the bookcases as though drawn by some magnetic force. Molly could have sworn she heard it rumble with pleasure as it reached the stacks.

The books seemed to glow as the fire consumed them, as though a light that had been held tight between their pages was now escaping out into the world.

The books were burning, and the library was consumed in chaos and flame.

The heat of the flames built, and Molly's whole body streamed with sweat. They had to move, but running was impossible. There wasn't enough fresh air to fill their lungs, and they coughed and spluttered more with every step. So, they stumbled together, crouching low and trying to find whatever air they could.

"There!" Molly cried, pointing toward the far wall on their

right. Through the clouds of smoke, she could dimly see a red exit sign glowing.

Jake cried out with relief, and they moved toward it.

Then the door flew open. Molly stopped short, staring in shock.

"Tyler?" she said, squinting through the smoke. "Is that you? What are you doing here?" Had the smoke inhalation hit her so hard she was hallucinating? Or had Andrew sent Tyler to come and help them get to safety?

Tyler didn't answer, but he smiled and beckoned. He held his hand out toward them, urging them to come. The emergency lights outlined his figure in brilliant flashes of red.

Jake took a step toward him and, acting on an instinct that she couldn't have explained with words, Molly grabbed onto his shoulder and yanked him back.

"No," she cried, and pulled him with her as she backed away.

Jake looked at her and taking in her expression, he turned instantly wary. His fingers squeezed hers. They backed away faster, moving toward the flames.

The smile on Tyler's face hardened and cracked. His lips pulled back from his teeth. He opened his mouth, and Molly knew he would use his voice.

Panic surged inside her, but there was no escape. She didn't know how to resist him; she had no way to protect Jake or herself.

Tyler's lips moved, and Molly braced herself, waiting for a force like gravity to fall on her and steal her will away.

But nothing happened. Above them, the alarms wailed, and Molly bit back a burst of bitter laughter.

The fire alarms saved them. Tyler's voice was drowned out by the noise.

Realizing he was deprived of his one true advantage, Tyler's face contorted with frustration and rage.

Then he pulled a gun from his waistband and fired at them.

"Fuck, fuck, fuck." Jake cursed. He pulled Molly low and

wrapped his arms around her shoulders as he tugged her behind a smoldering bookcase.

"There's got to be another exit on the other side!" he yelled, and Molly nodded agreement. They turned and began to run back the way that had come, keeping low to avoid both smoke and flying bullets. Molly glanced over her shoulder, and through a gap in the flames, she saw that Tyler was no longer alone. Two men had joined him, and they were picking their way carefully through the debris, their eyes probing the shadows. Searching for her and Jake.

Molly's chest burned. She and Jake leaned heavily against each other as they dragged themselves toward the other side of the building. Finally, they came into sight of the other red, emergency exit sign.

Two men stood beneath it, guns held loosely in their hands, their eyes probing the smoke-filled air, but not yet seeing them.

Molly wanted to scream, to throw things. She wanted to run right at the men who blocked their path and beat them senseless with her bare fists. But Jake was tugging at her arm again, as though they had someplace to go, as though they weren't trapped with the dark and the fire, locked in and hopeless.

Molly let him pull her, away from the men searching for them and over to the wall. It took her a second to realize what he was planning. But then, Jake picked up a nearby chair and, with a grunt of terrible effort, swung it above his head and brought it crashing down on the plate glass window that Molly hadn't even noticed was there. Immediately, she copied his efforts, picking up a chair of her own and battering the window with every ounce of strength she had left.

The problem was, she didn't have much strength left.

They swung again and again, Molly screaming with frustration as they beat against the glass, knowing that at any moment Tyler or one of the armed men he had brought with him might discover them. But after all the running and smoke inhalation, the window seemed nearly impossible to breach. Jake dropped his chair and kicked at the glass. Then he beat it with his fists.

Finally, the window cracked, the glass slicing Jake's fingers. With a terrible groan, it gave way at last.

Fresh night air streamed in through the opening, bathing Molly's face with blessed cold. Jake stepped up to the window, looking down to gauge the jump. Molly looked behind them but saw no sign of their pursuers. Maybe, she thought hopefully, the fire had gotten too intense, and they had given up. Maybe she and Jake could still get out.

"The jump's only two floors," Jake told her, speaking loudly so she could hear him above the victorious crackle of the flames. "We can make it."

"Quick," Molly agreed, and Jake held onto her arms to steady her as she climbed onto the window frame.

"I'm right behind you!" he called out in her ear.

Molly nodded. There was no time to hesitate, no chance to even think. She closed her eyes and jumped.

Two floors seemed like a lot, but it felt like only a split second passed between her feet leaving the windowsill and her body slamming down onto the ground. She crashed into a cluster of bushes, her ankle twisting painfully as branches tore at her face. The impact of the ground against her body forced what little air she had left out of her lungs.

Gasping and bleary-eyed, her fingers closed around something small and rounded that lay in the dirt under her. She clutched the object to her chest as she rolled over, the movement so painful that her vision swam. Then she lay still, looking through the leaves that sheltered her with anxious eyes. Waiting for Jake.

She saw him, standing in the window, his outline framed by the flames behind him. He was looking down, his eyes full of concern as they tried to find her in the darkness.

Molly knew she wouldn't be able to warn him.

She tried to call out. She reached up toward him, grasping at the air. Her words died, a useless croak in her throat.

"Behind you," she moaned, knowing it was too late, knowing he couldn't possibly hear her.

Tyler loomed at Jake's back. Molly watched . . . helpless . . . as Tyler's hand rose into the air, and he struck a savage blow to the back of Jake's head.

Jake crumpled instantly, and Molly's scream of outrage and horror died as little more than a choking cough as Tyler dragged Jake away from her, and back toward the flames.

MOLLY

"Carry her over to the trees," a voice whispered urgently. "If we're seen, things will get awkward fast."

Molly almost recognized the voice, but her head hurt too much for her to think clearly. Her vision was blurred. Still stunned from the fall, she could feel blood running hot down her cheek from where branches had cut her face. She still clutched the small, rounded object she had found beneath her in the dirt tightly, as though she could hold onto consciousness if she just kept her fingers closed tightly enough. She didn't even try to fight the arms she felt slipping around her legs and under her arms, hoisting her and carrying her quickly into the deeper shadows of a nearby cluster of trees.

In a daze, Molly lay still and looked at the stars through a gap in the leaves above her. The night was so clear. The stars were tiny pinpoints that seared the sky above her. Anger stirred deep inside her belly, its heat rising to match the intensity of the stars.

She thought she and Jake could run. She had really believed they could get out clean, and disappear into the night.

She had been wrong.

She had left Evie behind. Then Matt and Thia, too, when they got separated in the smoke. And now, she had ended up just like she did every time she had ever run from something: alone.

There was a time that being alone felt empowering. It felt safe. But now there was a huge hole deep inside her, where Jake was supposed to be. Her hand felt empty without his.

There are some kinds of evil you can't afford to turn your back on. She had made the wrong choice . . . and now Jake was paying the price for it. Molly felt Jake's absence like an aching wound in her side. She needed him, she realized, with a sudden burst of pain. She had thought she was the strong one, believed she was caring for him. But it had always been the other way around. She needed him beside her, looking up at her and seeing everything: the weakness she hid from everyone else, the scars she worked so hard to conceal. Seeing all of it and wanting her just the same.

And right now, who knew what Tyler might be doing to him?

At that thought, fury like fire ran through her and, suddenly, lying there in the dark, Molly didn't *want* to run anymore.

She sat up, pushing away the gentle hands that prodded her body, searching for injuries.

"Careful!" Matt cautioned, and Molly felt Thia's arm wrap around her shoulders, steadying her. "You hit your head pretty hard."

"Tyler's got Jake," Molly explained, her voice hoarse from smoke inhalation. Through the darkness, she could see Thia nod.

"We saw," she told Molly, glancing back up at the now empty window. "Tyler had at least two other people with him. They dragged Jake away."

"I've got to go find him," Molly said, moaning as she got to her feet.

Then she stilled. Now that she was standing, she realized the night was no longer quiet, the campus no longer dark and deserted. At least six fire engines were pulled up on the grass in front of the library. Barriers had been erected, and crowds of college students, many in their pajamas, pressed against them.

Molly could see the flames reflecting in their eyes as they stared at the burning building, eerily silent. Some were crying. Firefighters and rescue workers moved in tight teams, calling out instructions to each other, holding hoses that shot water in through the windows.

But the library was engulfed in flames.

It could have been beautiful. Orange and red and blue, the flames danced higher and higher as smoke twirled and spiraled into the night sky. The air was filled with the smell of paper burning.

It was then that Molly remembered the small object she still held tightly in her hand. In the orange and yellow glow from the fire, she opened her dirt-stained fingers and stared down at her palm.

Evie's USB key.

Her head ached, and her mind reeled as she struggled to understand the significance of what she held in her hand.

"What do we do now?" Thia asked, her voice thick with emotion.

Molly quickly shoved the USB key deep into her pocket. Her fingers tingled, as though it was filled with electric current.

"If Jake is still in that building . . ."

"He isn't." Molly shook her head so sharply that pain shot through her temples, but she didn't care. "I know it," she insisted, answering the uncertain look in Matt's eyes, cutting him off before he could even ask the question. She lay her hand against her chest. Jake told her when she had her panic attack that he had felt her need. She felt a pull now, deep inside. "He's alive . . . and he needs me." The pulling sensation tightened painfully. Molly winced. "He needs me *now*."

"That's why they took him," Matt said grimly, shaking his head. "Tyler knows Jake is linked to you. He's trying to force you to come to him."

"I don't care," Molly felt the need to rush to Jake's aid like a hook tugging deep on her insides. The pain of it made her voice sharp. "You guys go back to the tunnels. Get to safety. I'm going to find Jake." She grimaced with frustration. "I just have to figure out where to go."

"We aren't going to just leave you here," Thia protested, and Molly waved a hand to silence her.

"I'll be fine. I'm used to being on my own."

"You can't save Jake by yourself," Matt insisted, straightening up and brushing a bit of dirt from his hands. He raised his voice to cut off Molly's protest. "Listen, Molly. I get that you don't want to be a part of our mixed-up, dysfunctional, pseudo-family. I felt the same way for a long time, and my introduction to all of this was a lot smoother and less violent than yours. You're used to just relying on yourself—I get it. But you can sure as hell bet that Tyler isn't by himself. And you haven't learned how to control your voice yet. Whether you like it or not, you need our help."

Molly wanted to argue, but the words died in her throat as Thia came and lay a gentle hand on her shoulder.

"We want to help," Thia said, the corners of her lips curling up into a tired, but still mischievous smile. "And you may not have realized it yet . . . but I'm kind of a badass."

Molly hesitated, and Matt kicked the dirt in frustration.

"Come on, Molly. Quit wasting time," he urged her. "We're with you."

Molly stared at them, speechless. She literally could not think of a single word to say. She realized she was scrounging around in her mind for some excuse, anything, that would force them to leave her alone . . . and how did that make any sense? How could it be that, in her mind, letting them help her was scarier than walking into Tyler's trap alone?

"I guess it's just been a while," she finally stammered, "since I accepted help from *anybody*. It just seemed safer that way." Her hand crept up to her shoulder and traced the edges of the bracelet that hid her scars.

"I get it," Thia said. "Really, I do. I've been there. Life has given us hell, over and over again." She met Molly's eyes and grinned through the darkness. "I think it's high time we returned the favor."

The pull came again, tugging insistently deep inside Molly's chest. There was no more time for arguing.

"Okay," she agreed. "We'll go together. But how do we find him?"

"Just start moving," Matt told her. "Your link to Jake will pull you in the right direction. And we'll be right behind you."

Jake's need swelled inside her. Molly ran. Her feet flew across the grass in the darkness. The wind in her face was welcome and familiar. But she knew that, this time, things were different. This time she wasn't running away from something, but toward someone who needed her.

And this time, she wasn't alone.

JAKE

"You're surprisingly quiet, Dog. I didn't expect that. I took you for a squealer."

Tyler circled him slowly, and Jake locked his knees, waiting for the next blow to come. The most important thing, he thought to himself, was to stay on his feet. His vision was still blurry from the earlier blow to his head. If he went down, Tyler would start kicking him. And then he would be finished.

He had been pretty out of it while they dragged him down the stairs and into the maze of underground hallways that ran between the library and the other campus buildings. The room they finally brought him to seemed like part of an old cafeteria kitchen that hadn't been used for a long time. Dusty metal chairs were stacked in the corners, and in the periphery of Jake's vision, he could see Steele, perched on a counter, watching the proceedings with an expression of hostility.

"I'm getting booooored." Steele commented, in a sing-song voice that made Jake's skin crawl. He sat, swinging his legs back and forth beneath him like an impatient child. The muscles in Tyler's neck strained, and Jake took a little pleasure in knowing that, though he was the only one bleeding at the moment, Tyler was in almost as much trouble as he was.

Tyler's fist flew and, even though Jake had braced for the blow, pain still shot through him. He staggered backwards, biting down so hard on his lip that his teeth cut into his skin. Jake managed to stay on his feet. Tyler could beat on him all he wanted, but it wouldn't change a thing. Jake would hold his silence.

He didn't keep quiet out of pride. He could see that Tyler wanted him to cry out. Jake didn't know much about how his link to Molly worked. But he wasn't an idiot. He knew that anything Tyler wanted from him was something that he didn't want to give. In his gut, he knew that calling out would put Molly in more danger. Jake wouldn't let that happen.

He could take it. He would do it for her.

Jake turned his head to the side and spat blood onto the linoleum. He knew this couldn't go on forever. Sooner or later, he figured, Tyler would hurt him so badly that he would break. Or, he supposed, he might just die quietly. That was probably the better option.

"We've been going at this for a while now, Dog," Tyler leered, but his sneering voice couldn't hide the sweat beading on his brow or the way his eyes kept darting over his shoulder, in Steele's direction. "I keep waiting for Molly to come kicking down that door, screaming for me to keep my hands off her boy. She hasn't come. Could be she doesn't give a shit about you, which would make sense to me. But I think you're trying to block her. Are you?"

Jake kept his eyes focused on one of the tarnished metal chairs sitting in the corner of the room. It was easier than looking into Tyler's mocking expression, and Tyler was standing in front of him now, leaning in so close that his sour breath blew right in Jake's face.

Jake forced himself to stand tall, refusing to let his knees tremble. By now, he told himself, Molly had made it to the tunnels. She had probably found Matt and Thia, too. They would find a place to hide. He just had to hold out a little bit longer. Soon, Molly would be safe.

"Like I said: surprising." Tyler took a step back and tilted his head to the side, as though carefully selecting where to land the next blow.

"This is a waste of my time." Steele hissed. He slid down from the counter top, his black boots hitting the floor with a heavy thud. "Oh, I don't mean to interrupt you. By all means, continue beating this pathetic animal to death." He flicked his eyes in Jake's direction with a grimace of distaste. "But I have work to do." Steele started toward the door, and Tyler's Adam's apple bobbed violently as he swallowed hard, and it seemed that he had to struggle for a long moment before he could find his voice.

"But you . . . you had said I could come back with you," Tyler said, his tone caught somewhere between a plea and an accusation. "You promised that if I got you into the Refuge and helped you bring Andrew down, I could be one of you. No more hiding, no more living underground. You said I could be a Legacy!"

Steele froze, and turned back toward Tyler slowly, his eyes narrowed. He looked Tyler over coolly from head to toe. "Your genes are what they are," he said, his lips curling away from his teeth in distaste. "I've gone far in my research. I've accomplished a lot. But even I can't cleanse your genes . . . at least not yet. What I promised you was a place in my house. No more, no less."

Tyler nodded eagerly. "Yes," he said, "that's what I want."

Steele took a quick step closer, and Tyler flinched.

"Then *earn* it," Steele's voice dropped to a furious whisper. "I didn't want a fucking *tour* of the Refuge—I wanted to burn it to ashes! And I didn't just want to find Andrew . . . I wanted his research, his knowledge. If you want to claw your way up to respectability, then deliver the things you said you could. Clean up this mess. Finish this. I'll leave two of my men with you. That ought to be more than enough. When you're done, they'll bring you to our sanctum." His eyebrows climbed, and Jake could hear a faint rumble deep in Steele's chest. "If you can't finish this, then *you* will become the problem."

Steele turned away and pushed through the kitchen's swinging double doors, leaving Jake and Tyler alone in the kitchen.

For a second, Tyler stood, staring after Steele with a lost expression on his face. Then his expression crumpled and morphed into something deadly.

When he turned his eyes back to Jake, they were burning. His fist smashed into Jake's side, twisting as it went, digging under his rib cage. Jake felt something, probably a rib, snap. He stumbled, and caught himself on the corner of the counter, barely keeping himself from falling. He howled with anger and spun to throw himself at Tyler.

He hit an invisible wall.

He couldn't understand *why* he couldn't make himself hit Tyler. It felt like he had tried a hundred times in the last hour. But his body wouldn't obey his mind. It didn't matter how hard he fought it or how much he strained against the invisible chains that locked his hands to his side and left him standing helpless, fighting an invisible force.

Fighting and losing, again and again.

He could still curse, though.

"Fuck you!" he yelled, his face beet red and inches from Tyler's, his whole body shaking as he struggled to retaliate. Fury helped hold the fear at bay.

He spat in Tyler's face.

Tyler shook his head slowly and wiped the spittle from his check. "You've got no respect for your betters, boy." He held very still and watched Jake struggle, his voice low and dangerous. "No understanding of what your position is. You're just a slave, now. You know that? A piece of meat. An animal." Tyler's eyes were bulging. "And you've got no one but yourself to blame for that. I offered you a way out. If you'd done what I said, I'd have kept my word. I'd have given you the money, just like I promised. But you'd rather be some bitch's dog."

"It was *you*." Suddenly Jake didn't know why he had ever doubted it. He had thought he recognized Tyler's voice, wondered if it had been Tyler who slipped him the knife and told him to use it to kill Molly. But his memories were so fuzzy, so clouded with fear and drugs and pain. He hadn't been sure.

"Did you just figure that out now?" Tyler looked incredulous. "You're even stupider than I thought. Why do you think I picked you up off that dock? I'd been watching Molly for months. I knew she had a thing for you. I figured with you, she'd hesitate long enough for you to take her out. Would have saved me a shit-load of trouble, too. But you fucked it up." His fist smashed into Jake's midsection again.

"Why're you after Molly?" Jake gasped through the pain. "Why does she matter so much to you?"

"I don't answer questions from dogs," Tyler growled. He grabbed the back of Jake's head and slammed his face down onto the metal counter. The impact was so hard that Jake's knees buckled, and he crumpled to all fours, crouching on the ground, hanging his head low and fighting to stay conscious.

"Take off your shirt," Tyler ordered, and Jake cursed as he felt his hands moving to obey. He saw Tyler taking off his belt. "And this time, Dog, no more of the strong, silent type stuff. This time, I want our friend to hear you. I'm sick of this game. Time for her and I to have a little talk. I want you to scream. Hear me, boy? *Scream*."

MOLLY

"Which way now?" Thia called as they pounded down the hallway, but Molly didn't answer, she just threw herself around the bend and trusted that Matt and Thia would catch up. She grit her teeth as she ran, pushing her aching body to go faster. At first, she had felt Jake's need as a distant, amorphous pull somewhere deep inside her. Now she felt his need like flashes of a strobe light, lighting the darkness inside her, ringing out a pattern of desperation and alarm.

The thought of what must be happening to make his need so strong made her heart stutter, and her feet speed up even more.

The hallways under the college were dark and full of shadows, but Molly felt Jake's presence like a beacon. Down one hall, then another, until finally, a pair of stainless steel doors gleamed in the distance. Molly's heart swelled.

Jake was in there. She ran faster still, leaving Matt and Thia several paces behind.

She didn't even hear Matt's cry of warning; she was too focused on getting to that door. But suddenly his hands grabbed her from behind, and he pulled her to the floor, throwing his body down right beside her. Just as a spurt of gunshots boomed like cannon fire echoing through the vacant corridors.

Thia had dropped to the floor just behind them, but Molly saw her spring back to her feet after an instant, her eyes blazing as she faced the two figures who had stepped out of the shadows as they prepared to fire again.

"*Drop your weapons*!" Thia shrieked, her voice hitting an octave Molly had never heard before. She felt Thia's power pass over her like an icy wave, coursing toward their assailants with unstoppable force. Goosebumps spread across Molly's skin.

As the echoes of Thia's voice faded, for a moment the hallway rang with a silence so perfect and complete that Molly held her breath, not daring to break it.

Then, one of the men dropped his gun from numb fingers. The gun clattered as it fell. His pupils dilated, his hand still held out, numb and useless in front of him. His mouth dropped open. He stared at Thia, his eyes wide with wonder, his lip trembling with wordless emotion. He gazed at her with tears glistening in the corners of his eyes, like a man seeing the sun for the first time.

The other man scowled, his face twisting with contempt.

"Go to hell," he grunted with a small jerk of his head, shaking Thia's power off like a duck shaking water from its back. He raised his gun to fire again.

But, in the moment it had taken him to throw off her control, Thia had closed the distance between them. She grinned widely as she brought her fist up and punched him squarely in the face.

"Go," Matt yelled to Molly. He scrambled up from the floor and ran to help Thia, grabbing the man's arm and trying to pry the gun from his unwilling fingers. The first assailant blinked his eyes, emerging slowly from his dazed stupor.

Molly hesitated. "Are you sure?" she called to Matt, but she took a step closer to the double doors.

"Find Jake," Matt cried. "We can handle this."

Jake's need pulled at her insides again and, with a last worried glance over her shoulder, Molly turned and ran, leaving them behind as she sprinted the rest of the way down the hallway. After just a few steps, she couldn't hear the sounds of the struggle going on behind her anymore.

All she heard was Jake.

The sound was worse than screaming. It was guttural; deep. Not the sound of someone being beaten . . . the sound of someone being tortured.

She shoved doors open and ran inside, tripping and nearly falling over a metal chair next to the door. Her feet slid dangerously on the linoleum, and she fought to keep her balance. Looking down, her heart stuttered.

The linoleum was smeared with blood.

"Oh my God. Jake!"

Tyler stood over him, his hands on his hips, a look of smirking satisfaction on his face. Jake lay curled up on the floor, his face swollen and purple, his back a horror of bloody gashes.

She ran toward him, but Tyler stepped in front of her, blocking her path. He smiled at her widely.

Molly didn't slow. She slammed into him full force, knocking him back several paces, and swung out with her fist.

"You fucking bastard!" she screamed, as Tyler dodged her blow.

Jake was still conscious. Molly saw him roll a little onto his side, turning toward the sound of her voice, his eyes open, clear, and full of pain.

Flames of fury curled around Molly's spine, and a rush of rage swept through her. Everything else in the room seemed to fade. All she saw was the malicious smile glimmering in Tyler's eyes. All she felt was hatred.

Tyler grabbed her shoulders and pushed her away with a laugh.

"Finally," he growled. "It sure as hell took you long enough. I thought you had done the smart thing and taken off."

"I'm here now," Molly spit. "And you'll never touch Jake again, you God-damned, fucking monster."

Tyler's nostrils flared. His smile vanished, and his lips parted. Molly braced herself, waiting for his voice to assail her ears and attack her will.

Instead, he charged and punched her in the face.

If he had any reservations about hitting women, he hid them well. Molly deflected the worst of the blow, but his fist still caught her on the side of her face, hitting hard enough to make her vision wobble. He punched her again and again. Molly brought her knee up between his legs with savage force and had the satisfaction of hearing him cry out with pain. She let her fists fly, hitting him in the side of his stomach. But there was no question she was getting the worst of it.

Jake made a noise somewhere between a moan and a whimper. Molly's eyes flicked over to him, and she turned her face just enough to see him.

In that instant of distraction, Tyler swung his fist, and the blow landed squarely on her cheekbone. Pain flared white hot in Molly's mind, and the floor rose to meet her as she fell. She landed flat on her back on the bloody tile.

Instantly, Tyler was on top of her.

"You can't *breathe,* bitch!" he shouted, straddling her as he leaned down to shout right into her face. "You can't get no *air*!" His words were rhythmic, as though he were rapping. His voice had a deep, resonant quality, and each word ended with a hiss. ***"NO AIR!"***

An invisible force wrapped around Molly's neck. She opened her mouth, gasping for oxygen. Her back arched, and her fingers clawed at her throat as she tried in vain to pull intangible fingers away from her neck. But it was no help. Her airways were clamped shut. No air came through.

"I had to do it," Tyler whispered thickly into her ear, leaning his body down on top of hers so that the stubble around his mouth scratched her ear. "I know what you are. You're the key in the lock. You were going to change everything. I knew it, the first time I heard you sing." He stood up and looked down at her, something regretful in his eyes. "I couldn't let that happen."

He said something more, but Molly couldn't follow his words —she was too distracted by a terrible rasping, choking sound coming from somewhere nearby. A moment later, Molly realized that she was the one making the horrifying noises.

Through the haze of pain and confusion that quickly descended, she could feel Tyler standing over her. Watching her die. Her body spasmed. Jake sobbed from somewhere close by.

"Don't worry," Tyler said, reaching behind himself and pulling a gun from the waistband of his jeans, "I'll put your dog out of his misery." He turned his back on her and walked away, out of Molly's line of vision.

She felt like her soul was a bird darting around in the air outside her body, fluttering this way and that, peering around her with only mild interest. *I ought to be upset about something,* she thought. But everything was getting dark, and she couldn't remember what was wrong.

Her eyes closed, and suddenly she was on stage. Janice was beside her; Tim pounding on the drums behind them. They were singing one of her favorite songs. It was one she had written herself, staying up night after endless night, until the lyrics were perfect, and the song said everything just as she wanted. Janice threw her arm around Molly's shoulder, and they leaned in, sharing the same mic. In front of the stage, Jake stood, gazing at her. Smiling.

Joy soared inside her as the words she knew so well flowed smoothly from her lips, filling the air, reverberating off the walls. The music swelled around her like a living thing that wrapped warm arms around her, pulling her close in a joyful embrace.

And then Molly could feel the warmth inside.

The music uncurled inside her chest, as though it had always been waiting there, deep inside her, sleeping fitfully and waiting for her to call to it. Now, Molly reached out to it and felt it swell inside her like sunlight rising. The sound of it rang in her ears, more beautiful than anything she could remember. A joy she had never felt before swept through her, a gentle tide that lifted her and carried her away.

The sound got louder and louder, each word the clang of a great bell tolling, resonating through every inch of her body; announcing the break of a new day.

The music boomed, the sound of it crashing through her like cleansing waves. The noise drowned everything out: her fear, the pain, the swirling desperation at her core . . . even Tyler's command. The words of the song churned in her brain, and peace washed over her.

Molly breathed.

Air leaked into her lungs, but she hardly noticed it. In her mind, she was still on stage with Janice.

The air came again. The song was so strong inside her and its strength coursed through her body, filling her veins, soothing her throat . . . opening her lungs. Molly pulled air in, and awareness flowed back to her.

She opened her eyes.

Tyler's head turned, and his eyes widened. Slowly, Molly rose to her feet.

There was a moment, a single moment when he could have acted. He could have brought his gun up and fired before Molly could have done a thing. But Tyler's mouth fell open with surprise, and in the fraction of a second that it took him to understand what was happening, Molly was coming at him, flying forward, her eyes blazing.

In that instant, all the beauty of the song inside her flashed golden, and her joy transformed into fury that quivered inside her like an arrow drawn and notched.

"*STOP*!" she screamed at Tyler, with the force of her whole soul in her throat. "*Don't move!*"

Tyler's body might as well have turned to stone. He stood immobile, his gun useless in his hands. Molly picked up a nearby metal chair and brought it crashing down full force on Tyler's face and shoulders. There was an ugly thud, and the snap of bones breaking. The gun was knocked from his grip and slid away on the slick floor.

"What did Jake ever do to you?" she screamed at him as he fell. She brought the chair crashing down on him again. "FUCKING bastard!"

The blood pounded in her ears, and as she raised the chair above her head, she did not care at all that the next blow would probably kill him.

The double doors burst open behind her, and Andrew stumbled into the room. He stopped short when he saw Molly standing over Tyler's limp form.

"Wait," Andrew cried from the doorway, holding out a hand in her direction. His perfect hair was disheveled, his shirt stained with dirt and blood. The left side of his face was covered with a dozen small cuts that were still bleeding, as though he had been struck by shattered glass. "Don't kill him," Andrew said. The words were not an order, but a plea. "Not yet. He's a traitor, and he's got it coming. But there are things he knows."

Molly looked down at Tyler. Already her anger was ebbing. She let the chair fall from her fingers with a terrible crash.

"You can have him," she told Andrew, turning away from Tyler's crumpled form with a shudder. "I came for Jake."

She ran to Jake's side and knelt beside him.

"I'm okay," he told her, sitting up with a groan.

"You don't look okay," Molly whispered. She reached out for him but hesitated. She wasn't sure how to touch Jake without hurting him.

"What, this?" Jake tried to smile reassuringly, though the effect was ruined by the bloody split of his lip. "This is nothing. I've been in worse scraps than this." He put his hand on her shoulder for support and staggered onto his feet.

"Are you sure you're okay to get up?" Molly asked anxiously, rising beside him and wrapping her arm around his waist. "Maybe you should let Matt take a look at you first."

Jake grimaced, shaking his head. "Are you kidding?" he asked, his voice rasping painfully. "I'm just gonna walk this off." He wobbled dangerously, and Molly tightened her hold on him so he wouldn't topple back down.

"Hey, let me help you out there!" Matt called, running in through the door. His left eye was swollen nearly shut, but otherwise, he seemed unharmed. Thia rushed in just a step behind him. Several other Echoes, whom Molly recognized vaguely, also hurried into the room and clustered around Andrew in a tight, anxious knot.

Matt peered into Jake's eyes and ran an expert hand over his skull and down his sides. "How bad is he?" Molly asked, trying to read the expression on Matt's swollen face.

"Nothing broken," Matt announced after a brief pause. "Though he might have a cracked rib or two. He's got some healing to do, and we'll have to make sure those wounds on his back don't get infected. But he'll be okay."

Thia joined the group of battered Echoes huddling around Andrew, as though his shadow might offer them some degree of protection. "Please tell me we aren't the only ones who made it out," she said, leaning toward him. All the fight that Molly had seen shining in her eyes just a little bit ago seemed to have fizzled and disappeared.

Andrew sighed heavily and pushed his disheveled hair out of his eyes.

"Most people made it to safety." Thia closed her eyes and let out a long, shaky sigh of relief. "We haven't made contact with everyone yet, but it seems like Steele was pretty focused on tracking me down."

"What happened?" Thia asked him.

"Tyler turned traitor. I don't know why. Yet." Andrew glanced down at Tyler, who still lay unconscious on the floor. "He gave Steele the location of the refugee, and he knew all our evacuation plans. We," he gestured to the people gathered around him, "were holed up in a room right under the tunnels. Tyler led Steele straight to us. We were cornered, and did the only thing we could," Andrew shrugged. "We fought back. We lost some good people, and Steele is stronger than any of us alone. But it turns out they weren't really expecting a fight—they were expecting a slaughter. They didn't like it much when we started fighting back. We outnumbered them; and we were fighting with nothing to lose. When they couldn't get the job done after all, they left. At first, I thought they'd just quit and gone home. But then I realized that isn't Steele's style. And I knew that, with a voice like yours," he nodded to Molly, "you'd be at the top of Steele's hit list. By the time I did figured out where you were, I thought we'd be too late. I got here as fast as I could. But . . ." Andrew rubbed the back of his neck ruefully. "I guess you didn't need saving quite as much as I expected."

"What are we going to do now?" Thia asked, gazing up at Andrew with a doe-like expression.

But Andrew wouldn't meet her eyes. Thia looked over at Matt, and then to Molly. "We worked so hard to hide ourselves," she said, "but they found the one place where we were safe. The only place we weren't hunted. Where can we even run to now?"

No one answered, and Molly could feel fear and desolation mounting in the room. Even Matt was staring at the floor.

"That's why we don't run," Molly said into the silence, the words spilling out before she was even sure she wanted to speak. Everyone turned to stare at her. She took a deep breath, threw her head back and looked slowly around the room. "Running won't fix this. It would weaken us. We'd have to split up, and Steele would hunt us down one by one. Our strength is in our numbers; we've already seen that tonight." She turned to Andrew. "You already showed them once that we're stronger than they thought. And, in a different way, we did too." She nodded to Matt and Thia while pulling Jake a little closer against her side. "Now we have to teach Steele and the rest of the Legacies that lesson over and over again until they believe it. Until they stop thinking of us as prey. We have to stand our ground."

Molly glanced over at Jake. His eyes were bright and burning and, as he listened to her, a slow smile spread across his bruised face. "Steele is a monster. People like that don't stop hurting people unless you make them. Thia is right; your home isn't a Refuge anymore." Molly reached into her pocket and pulled out Evie's USB key. She held it up so everyone could see it. "But you can make it into a Fortress."

Molly swallowed hard. She wasn't sure she was doing the right thing by giving them the USB key, but there didn't seem to be a whole lot of good options. And Steele had to be stopped. "This was Evie's," she told Andrew. "I'm not totally sure what's on here. But she thought it was important, and I'm betting that something on it can help."

Andrew paled and took the USB key from her hand with wide eyes.

"Why would Evie have kept this from me?" he asked, holding it in two hands, as though it was heavy with all the secrets it held.

Molly shook her head. Thinking of Evie hurt her heart. "She believed that she could find someone else to take Steele on. But it looks like it's up to us."

Matt was still standing on Jake's other side. He leaned forward, craning his head around to peer at Molly quizzically.

"You know," Matt said, a sly smile on his face, "I can't help but notice you seem to be using the word 'us' quite a lot. Almost as though you consider yourself a part of our dysfunctional little family."

Molly hesitated.

"Are you planning on coming back with us, then?" Matt prodded. "'Cause to me, you don't look like someone who's about to sulk off into the shadows. You look like somebody who's itching for a fight."

"We need you," Andrew hurried to add. "If this has the information on it that I'm hoping it does," he held the USB key up a little higher, "it won't do us much good without you."

"Come with us," Thia urged with a smile. "You're family now."

Molly couldn't help but smile back. She looked over at Jake, who had been watching her with quiet intensity the whole time.

"What do you think?" she asked in a whisper, knowing full well that everyone in the room could still hear. "What should we do?"

Jake shrugged and then winced a little when the movement hurt. "I'm with you," he said. "I go where you go, it's as simple as that. Doesn't matter much to me where that is." He nodded his head in Thia's direction. "I will admit, though," he added with a smile, "she does make an awfully good burger."

Molly leaned against Jake's side, letting his warmth seep into her. Deep inside, she could still feel her song, vibrating at her core, strong and ready. She looked at Andrew, holding the USB key; at Matt and Thia, standing with their arms thrown loosely around each other. At the other Echoes, whose names she didn't know, but who shared something with her that was strange and powerful enough to intertwine their fates.

"Okay," she said, feeling less alone than she had in a very, very long time. "I'm in. Let's go home."

EPILOGUE: BEA

Bea hadn't expected to wake. The surprise made it harder.

She was coughing before she was conscious, and at first forcing the water out of her lungs took her entire being, every ounce of her strength. She retched, and the water poured out of her, stinging and burning as it went, clear when it hit the ground.

Ground!

She lay on a bed of wet moss, the sun shining fiercely on her still-bare skin, the ocean unseen but audible, crashing against some unknown shore not far away. Bea pushed herself up.

Then she saw him.

"Holy fucking Christ!" she exclaimed. "I died!"

The angel smiled.

Bea steadied herself, propping her hands against the soggy ground and staring up at him. He was glorious. The sun was shining behind him; his shoulder-length pale hair glowed gold. He wore no shirt, and the muscles of his arms and smooth chest were like perfect arches carved in pale white stone. He wore skin-tight pants of black leather, and crouched there, in front of her, his face creased with concern. But his eyes were smiling. Behind him, his black wings billowed out into the sky. They were strong, smooth black leather, matching the leather of his pants. She could see the veins that ran through his wings, round and thick as her arm. A single small, sharp claw curled from their edges on either side. His eyes were dark and kind. His chin covered with blond stubble.

It took her a moment to process it all.

"I *am* dead, right?" she asked at last, suddenly uncertain. The angel smiled and shook his head. No.

Bea frowned, not convinced.

"Are you an angel?"

He smiled broadly now, the lines of worry on his face smoothing out. He shook his head again.

This made sense to Bea. She had never imagined angels in skin-tight leather pants. Not that she didn't like them. She couldn't help staring at him, and admitting to herself that she liked him, and his pants, very much.

She rubbed her face, ran her hands over her sore neck and her scratched bare chest and arms. She pressed her palms against her scalp. Brown stubble was sprouting there, the twin of the stubble on the angel's chin. She looked up at him again, and all around her, but the scene did not change.

"Who are you?" she asked. But the angel did not respond. He looked at her.

"Don't you talk?"

Slowly, warily, he shook his head.

"Wait a minute, wait a minute." Bea felt slightly dizzy, and her head throbbed where it had hit against the boat's wreckage while she floundered in the water. She closed her eyes as she tried to reason it all out.

"A gorgeous man who has no shirt, but has wings. Who can't talk . . . but can only listen." She shook her head and opened her eyes.

"Crap," she said. "I *am* dead!"

The angel laughed now, opening his mouth to flash perfect, white teeth. But he laughed without making a sound.

Then he stood up and, very slowly, offered her his hand.

* * *

Molly's story continues in Magic Cries . . .

Don't miss the next part of Molly's Journey . . .

Available now on Amazon!!
http://www.miriamgreystone.com/getbook2

Did you enjoy this book? Reviews are vital to a book's success. Please consider leaving a brief review; even a few short lines will help this book find new readers. Thank you!

http://www.miriamgreystone.com/MagicCallsKindle

ACKNOWLEDGMENTS

Many people have been a huge part of bringing this book to life. Thank you to my wonderful family, for their support and enthusiasm through all the ups and downs that are part of the writing and publishing process. My husband and children have cheered me on and encouraged me when I felt overwhelmed or discouraged. My sister has read multiple drafts and been a true support for me in every step of this process. My father's sincere pride in my accomplishments means the world to me. My mother was a big part of this book's development, reading early drafts and giving me limitless encouragement. I am happy that she was able to read the manuscript, even though she is not with us now to see the book come out.

I have benefited immeasurably from the advice and guidance of my critique partners, Grace and Michelle. Their friendship, and their patience with me as I struggle through the writing process, has been a vital part of my growth as a writer. I honestly don't know where I would be as an author if I didn't have them in my life.

Michelle Rascon did an amazing job of editing this book, and I am very, very grateful to her. Clarissa Yeo surpassed all my hopes in creating a truly breathtaking cover.

And a huge thank you to all the people who read this book, who fall in love, as I have, with the characters on these pages. Thank you for caring, for reading, and for sharing your enthusiasm. You make all of this possible, and I am incredibly thankful to you.

Love,

Miriam

ALSO BY MIRIAM GREYSTONE:

The Echoes Series

Magic Calls

Magic Cries

Magic Sings – *Coming soon!!*

The Outcast Mage Series

Truthsight

Winter's Mage

Be sure to join my Insiders list to get free sneak peeks, new release notices, and giveaways! Join here: http://www.miriamgreystone.com/connect-with-me/

Printed in Great Britain
by Amazon

58833386R00130